Grayson Davis 6.99

Dream Saver

Michelle Izmaylov

Illustrated by
Alexander Kanchik
and
Anthony Garvin

Dream Saver

by

Michelle Izmaylov

ISBN-10: 0-9778793-0-5
ISBN-13: 978-0-9778793-0-4
Library of Congress Catalog Control Number: 2006933340

Mercury Publishing, Inc.
2526 Mt.Vernon Road, Suite B137
Dunwoody, Georgia 30338

www.mercurypublishinghouse.com

Book Design
by
Faith Instructional Design, Inc.
www.faithid.biz

Dedication

With love to Alex, Gina, and Nicole,
for never letting me down and listening to countless
revisions, time and time again.
Thank you for believing.

Book One

Chapter One

"Mom," asked Taylor, "why are there so many people here?"

"What people? Why, there's no one here except us," answered her bewildered mother as she bent over the girl . . .

∽ ∽ ∽

The sky exploded in a blaze of sea and light. The sun smiled down from the azure expanse far above the emerald land. Below, a silvery sports utility vehicle flashed among the hills and cast sparkling shadows along its boundless path. It was a perfect day for a move, and it seemed impossible for anything to go wrong. *Today, everything will change!* Taylor stuck her head out of the back seat window, letting the breeze catch her dark hair and sending it streaming out behind her. *New house, here I come!* she thought.

The weather seemed to be celebrating with her. The sun was glowing high above, and there was not a single cloud to be seen. There was a gentle and cool wind that made all the trees and plants wave and dance as if welcoming Taylor to her new home. Up ahead, Taylor could see her brand new house on a smooth, gently rolling hill. The light brown bricks and gray stone reflected the sun to give them a beautiful sparkle. The house reminded Taylor of an ancient castle that had been restored like new, and the best part was that this castle was her home!

The Creekmore's silver SUV pulled into the driveway. The automobile stopped before double garage doors. Taylor stared at the doors in awe. They had been expertly carved out of solid wood and painted by a true artist's hand. The doors barely creaked as they rose up and out of sight. The vehicle drove slowly into the garage, and Taylor felt her heart leap as she entered her home for the first time.

Taylor and Amanda, the two daughters of Alex and Sarah Creekmore, jumped out of the SUV. They were both very excited about the move, and it was impossible to decide who was happier. The two girls ran to the back of the vehicle and picked up one box each. Holding the boxes carefully so that they wouldn't break anything, the girls carried them into the house.

Taylor let out a great gasp as she entered the house. The grand staircase, sweeping foyer, hardwood floors, and the large, open rooms took her breath away. She greeted the house with her thoughts. *What a beautiful house you are! I knew I would love you!* She looked around and was pleased to see that the moving company had already brought the furniture from their old house.

Taylor looked down at the box she was carrying. It was labeled with her name and the word "Books." Remembering where her mother had said her room was, she quickly ran up the stairs and made her way to the last room on the second floor. When she reached her bedroom door, she screamed with joy, "Oh, wow! I can't believe this!" The room was the exact opposite of her room in their old house. Taylor's old room was dark and cramped, with only enough room for a bed and a small bedside table. This room was bright, large and comfortable. Taylor knew she could fit all of her stuff in this room and have plenty of space left over.

She stepped from the hardwood floor of the hallway onto the soft, plush carpet of her new room. Taylor lowered the box of books onto the floor, then straightened out and stretched her stiff back. Sitting in the SUV all day had not been easy, especially for a girl who liked being outside.

At that moment, eight-year-old Amanda ran into the room and flung herself on her older sister. Taylor staggered under her sister's weight and fell to the carpet with Amanda laughing on top of her. Looking annoyed, Taylor pushed the young nuisance away and said, "Amanda, please stop."

The younger girl stopped laughing and said, "Mom and Dad are waiting for you. It's time to eat." With that, Amanda skipped through the door and out of sight.

Taylor was quite trustworthy, although she was only fourteen years old. Her parents often trusted her to cook the evening meal and to look after her younger sister.

Amanda was quite attached to her big sister. In fact, given the choice, Amanda would stay with Taylor from dawn to dusk. Normally, this would be an easy task, but there was a slight catch. Amanda loved to play. She loved to play games more than anything else in the whole world. She stuck to Taylor like glue because she knew she could force her older sister to play with her. Whenever Taylor refused, Amanda ran to her mother, crying and complaining.

Of course, Amanda hadn't really cried for a few years now, but she knew if she wailed for a few minutes, her parents would give her whatever she wanted. The girls' mother, Sarah, usually encouraged Amanda to watch a movie or read a book first. Then, she would ask Taylor to entertain her sister. Sarah could not play with Amanda because she ran her own business and was almost always busy with clients. Their father had the same problem. He was usually at his appliance store. So Taylor was the only person in the house who could amuse Amanda.

Taylor raced downstairs and found her way to the kitchen, following the wonderful smells coming from the dinner table. A glass table stood in the center of the eating area of the large kitchen. An island counter with a surface of black marble sat in the middle of the kitchen. The rest of the countertops were also made of the black marble. An enormous stainless steel Sub-Zero stood in an inlet made for the refrigerator. The floor in the kitchen was of the same hardwood that ran through most of the house.

"Taylor, come, sit. It's time to eat," Alex called.

Running to the table, Taylor jumped into her chair, picked up her fork and speared a dumpling. Sarah glanced over at Taylor and smiled.

"So," Alex asked, "how does everyone like the new house?"

"Oh, it's absolutely wonderful! I love my new room! The house is amazing!" Taylor shouted.

Alex chuckled, then turned to Amanda. "And do you like it?"

Amanda puffed out her cheeks. "When is the playroom going to be finished? I'm losing playtime!"

"We've only been in the house for half an hour and the only thing you can worry about is the fact that you're losing play time because the playroom isn't finished?" Taylor giggled at her sister. Amanda pouted at her, and the entire family laughed at her puffed-up expression.

Suddenly, Taylor's eyes lit up as she remembered something. "Well, I know something that's much more interesting than a playroom. I have a surprise for everyone. I've started writing a brand new book!"

"Oh, really!" Amanda exclaimed with interest. "What's it about?"

"The book starts with a girl who finds a pocket watch buried in the dirt near her house. When she opens the watch, she discovers it has sixteen buttons instead of hands and numbers. She presses one of the buttons and is whisked off to another world!"

"Like one with unicorns?" Amanda squealed.

"Sort of. The girl . . . her name's Nicole . . . does meet a dragon later, but it's more a traveling-to-different-planets thing. Anyway, her task is to seek out four enchanted crystals that represent the four elements of life—earth, water, fire, and air—to save Earth. To do it, she'll need the help of two aliens, her dragon, a stallion of legends, and other amazing creatures."

"Wow!" Amanda breathed.

"And I've already picked out a name for the book, too—*The Galaxy Watch*!"

Amanda opened her mouth to speak again, but her mom silenced her with a sharp look. "Well, Taylor, that is exciting, and we're very proud of you. Your new book sounds very interesting. But right now, it's getting late, and we have a lot of unpacking to do tomorrow. I think we should all get to bed early and have a good night's rest. You can tell us more about it tomorrow."

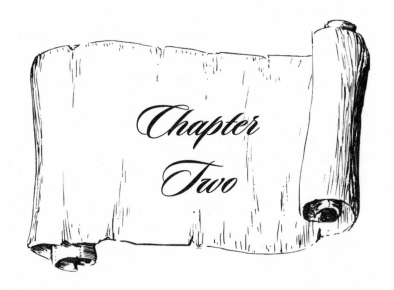

Chapter Two

The first rays of the morning sun squeezed through a crack between two pearly-white blinds in Taylor's room. The rays danced on her face, causing her to open her eyes.

"But why so early?" Taylor, yawning widely, asked the rays. She lay back down on her bed and pulled the covers over her face to shield her eyes from the light, but soon lost all interest in sleeping.

Taylor quickly showered and dressed in a pink, short-sleeved shirt and blue, zippered jeans. She brushed her teeth carefully and washed her face before going into the hallway. Suddenly, she heard a sniffing sound coming from the first floor. Taylor ran swiftly but quietly down the stairs, not wanting to wake up anyone else. She listened carefully to pinpoint the source of the sniffing. On the very bottom step sat her tiny Yorkshire terrier puppy, Don. He was trying to get up the stairs but was so small that he was having no luck. Taylor laughed at the puppy and picked him up gently. She carried the little dog to the front door, put on his leather leash and, together, they walked outside into the morning sun.

The rising sun cast golden shadows upon the shiny roofs, the grand gardens, and the wide streets of Taylor's new subdivision. She walked along the street, examining the neighboring homes. There were only forty-six houses in the subdivision. Each mimicked a French castle. The house to the right of hers had white brick walls and a tall, curved window above the carved wooden door. The house next to the white one had gray stone walls and a swirling tower on its left front corner. Most of the houses were already occupied, but several were still under construction. Taylor loved the wide variety of architecture that made the houses unusual and seemingly ancient. It was incredible to think of all the lives that went on behind the walls of these houses, away from prying eyes.

The little puppy ran for the grass. Taylor laughed and called out to him, "Be careful, Don!"

Don barked back in reply, and then landed on his stomach in the grass. Don was so small that he vanished in the tall stalks, and Taylor had to fish him out before they could continue their walk. The puppy loved all of the Creekmores, but Taylor was his very favorite. She groomed him, fed him, and walked him. She also played games like tug-a-bone and fetch with him. Don rubbed against her leg and gave another short bark of joy. Taylor stroked her hand along his back.

Suddenly, Taylor heard rustling coming from behind her. She whirled around and came face-to-face with a boy. He looked to be about sixteen and had short, straight dark hair and an athletic build. He seemed friendly, but what drew Taylor's attention the most were his brown, sparkling eyes. Although they looked ordinary, she could tell there was something deep behind his gaze. The boy waved at her.

"Hi, princess! You must be our new neighbor."

"Yes . . ."

"Then we should get to know each other. My name is Erik. What's yours?"

Taylor did not expect to meet anyone this early in the morning. She could feel her face redden as she answered, "Taylor, and, you guessed it! My palace is indeed in this kingdom."

"Well, I'm so glad that there's some young blood in this place now. There wasn't anyone my age to hang out with before."

As Erik turned, Taylor noticed something flashing in his jean pocket. "What's that?" she asked curiously.

"This?"

The young man pulled a long, golden chain from his pocket and handed it to the girl. A gold pocket watch was at the end of the chain.

"My grandfather made this for my mother. I just borrowed it so I would know when to head home. I broke my wristwatch a few days back," he said.

"Your grandfather . . ."

"He's a professional jewelry artisan."

Erik glanced at the watch and gasped. He looked at Taylor and smiled. "I guess I'll see you around. I've got to go." Erik took off down the street as Taylor gazed at his retreating back. The meeting with Erik left her absorbed in her thoughts until Don tugged at his leash. She turned to head home with the little puppy running clumsily behind her.

Back at home, everyone was still sleeping soundly. Taylor closed the door quietly, unlatched the leash from Don's collar, and walked to the kitchen. There, she took a box of oatmeal from the cupboard over the sink, poured it into a pan, added milk and placed it on the stove, covering the pan with a lid. As soon as it was cooked, she shifted the pan from the stove to a trivet on the kitchen counter and waited for it to cool.

What should I do while everyone is sleeping? Taylor wondered. She decided taking a look around the rest of the house would be the best way to pass the time. She began on the first floor in the dining room, which had a large, elegantly carved wooden table in the center and a china buffet filled with plates. From the dining room, she walked into the living room. A set of leather furniture was already in place. Behind the sofa, which stood against the wall, were three wide, two-story windows that extended all the way to the ceiling! After marveling at the windows, Taylor walked into the library. There were many built-in bookshelves along the walls. *Wow!* she thought. All the bookshelves were already filled with books. *When did Dad have time to do all this?*

When Taylor left the library, she decided to look around upstairs. She climbed the steps quietly, trying hard not to wake anyone. She walked past Amanda's bedroom and the laundry room. She was about to turn back when she noticed a door at the far end of the hall. *I wonder where this leads? How did I miss this before?*

Taylor tiptoed to the door and turned the handle. The room was very dark, and the lack of windows made it eerie. Taylor walked inside and felt the wall for a light switch. Finding it, she flipped it upward, causing the room to flood with light. The room was not finished. Boxes and wood shavings littered the floor. A few cans of white paint stood in the corner, and a blueprint of the house lay spread in the middle of the floor. Taylor walked farther into the room, but suddenly felt the floor shudder beneath her. She felt herself falling down and down and down . . .

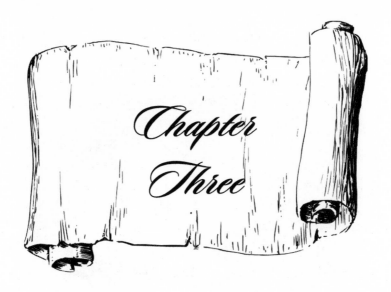

Chapter Three

"But I hear voices, Mom. Where am I?"

Taylor lay on a soft bed. Her mother kneeled beside the bed, looking worried. "Darling, you're in the hospital. You just had an operation. There's no one here except the two of us."

"But I hear voices, Mom."

Sarah stood up, and Taylor heard her run out of the room. The door closed softly behind her, leaving Taylor alone. She listened as her mother talked to someone in the hall. Taylor heard her name a few times, as well as the words "hallucination" and "delusion." The voices moved closer to her door, and she was able to catch more of the conversation.

"Patients experience different side effects from the narcotics. They may have hallucinations, which is what I believe your daughter is having."

Taylor heard her mother gasp. Seeing the scared look on Sarah's face, the doctor added, "But don't worry. It all passes in due time. Please stay calm. There is no need to worry. I promise it will pass."

Taylor heard the door reopen and the soft footsteps of her mother returning. Sarah brushed her hand against Taylor's cheek.

"I just talked with the doctor. He said that hearing voices is a normal side effect of the pain medicine. The voices will pass."

"But what happened to me, Mom?"

"You don't remember?" Sarah asked.

"No. Nothing. Nothing at all."

"You fell from the upstairs storage closet into the garage. The floorboards collapsed beneath you. You suffered a head injury that affected your vision. The doctors had to operate to relieve the pressure on your optic nerve. But that's all behind us now. Tomorrow, they will remove the bandage from your eyes."

As her mom finished, Taylor remembered the closet and falling through the floor. She lay in the bed with the bandage wrapped tightly over her eyes, listening to the gentle, murmuring voices and conversations of the many people around her, although she could not see them.

The voices became softer and farther away . . .

The door to Taylor's room creaked open, and the doctor peeked inside.

"So, how is our patient?" he asked gently.

"Sleeping," Sarah replied.

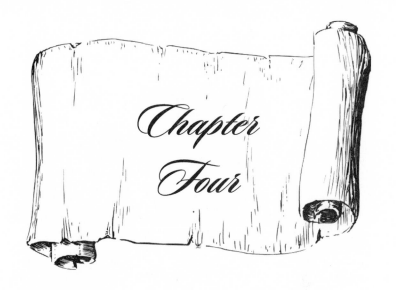

Chapter Four

"Off the road!"

Taylor, dressed poorly in a ragged dress and torn, mud-caked shoes, slopped through the mud. Her family ran beside her, also dressed in old, torn clothes. All around them trudged villagers, most clothed like Taylor's family, but some men were without even so much as a shirt. *We may be poor,* Taylor thought, *but at least we're still alive.*

Her entire village had been forced to flee because of a terrible plague. A disease that wiped out entire families had infected one of the villagers. At first, the only visible signs of the disease were black spots all over the man's body. Many of the villagers suspected it might be the plague but kept quiet, not wanting to scare anyone if they were wrong. But the infected man grew weaker and paler by the hour. When he finally died in the night, the village medicine woman confirmed what most of them feared. The Black Plague had struck.

On the day following the man's death, everyone left the village. Leaving their belongings to rot in their abandoned homes, they marched onto the muddy road. The villagers had traveled in this fashion for a while now, sleeping beside the road when it grew dark and wandering in search of a new home during the day.

"Off! Off the road!" A rider galloped past them, his horse spraying mud in the air.

"That is Erik, the count's son," Taylor heard a quiet voice beside her. She turned to look at a strange man with a dirty, tangled beard, matted hair, and ragged clothes. He motioned toward the young man on the stallion and spoke again.

"I am a monk," he said. "I am going south. I am one of the few who escaped death, even though the Black Death infected me."

"You survived?" Taylor gasped. "Then there is a cure for the disease!"

"Yes, but only if you are very fortunate."

"Please tell me, what causes this disease?"

"I don't know. Perhaps God sent it as payment for our sins."

"But isn't war already enough punishment? Taking away our loved ones is a dreadful toll," a woman added to the conversation. She was about forty years old and wore a dirty dress. "Do we really need the Black Plague as well?"

"Maybe we do need it. Who knows?" the monk replied. "But we are forced to go south now. Everyone who stays here will die, if not of the Black Plague, then of hunger."

"So you really believe that God sent these trials, the war, and this disease?" asked Taylor.

"No one knows," the monk answered. "Perhaps, this is a warning to us, our children, our children's children, and all future generations: Be careful. Respect and love each other. Otherwise, terrible things may befall you."

A rider suddenly appeared, pulling back on his horse's reins. The horse snorted and turned around. This time, the horse did not gallop, but walked slowly toward the refugees.

"Wait a moment. What is this I hear of a disease?" the rider asked.

Taylor curtsied low before the count's son and said, "We have fled our village because of a terrible plague. We have nowhere to go now."

"And how long have you been traveling?"

"A few weeks now, I think. It's hard to keep track of the days when death is close behind you and the stench of fear is always with you."

The young man on the horse nodded and gave the refugees a quick look.

"Listen! I can help all of you. My name is Erik. My castle is up ahead. Halt there, and you will be given food, drink, and a warm place to rest. Fear not! The Black Plague has not yet looked into this corner of the kingdom." As an afterthought, he added, "And I am sorry for yelling at you to get off the road before."

"But what about you?" Taylor asked softly. "Do you not fear the terrible plague that we may bring with us?"

Erik's eyes met with the girl's for a moment, and they held each other's gaze. Taylor thought she saw something distant stir and sparkle within his eyes. Then, he smiled and said, "If any of you had been infected, you would have been long dead. A few weeks are enough to weed out the ill. Either way, I would never forgive myself if I left you on the road to die."

As Erik spurred his horse and galloped down the dirt road, Taylor could not help but feel the somersault her heart turned in her chest.

Chapter Five

"Well, how about we let her rest a little longer?" the doctor suggested.

"Or maybe it would be better to wake her up?" Sarah asked. "She is sleeping very fitfully."

Taylor recognized her mother's voice and opened her eyes. "I'm not sleeping anymore. Are they going to remove the bandage now?"

"If you don't mind," the doctor said.

"No, not at all! I keep hearing voices. I want to finally see the faces of the many people I've been hearing."

Sarah exchanged a worried look with the doctor. He shrugged his shoulders and placed a hand on Sarah's.

"Don't worry," he said. "This sometimes happens. It will pass."

The doctor opened the door and called one of the nurses. The nurse walked in and stood beside Sarah. The doctor told Sarah to hold Taylor while he and the nurse removed the bandage. Taylor heard the soft swish of cloth as the bandage came off her eyes. When she tried to open them, she saw only a brilliant white light that caused her to gasp. Everything around her seemed to double, but slowly the room came into view and the light faded. Taylor looked around excitedly, wanting to see the people she had heard. But there was no one in the room except her mother, the doctor, and the nurse.

"So, are you convinced now that we are the only people in this room?" Sarah asked.

"Yes," Taylor replied sadly. "I guess I just dreamed that I heard voices."

Her mother smiled sweetly at her and turned to leave, saying she would update Alex on how Taylor was doing. When the adults had finally gone, Taylor spoke aloud to the voices that she heard.

"I may not be able to see you, but I know you're here. Please, answer me."

For a second, the room became very quiet. The voices stopped suddenly, and the only sounds were the scuttling of feet outside in the hospital corridor and the soft patter of rain on the window.

Then, one voice spoke. "We did not know that you could hear us. I know your name, Taylor. Don't be afraid. I can explain everything to you."

Taylor gasped in surprise. "So there is someone here! Who . . . who are you?"

"It may be difficult for a young child such as yourself to understand, but I will try to make it clear for you. We are the spirits of creatures—all creatures, not just you humans—who have passed away. But don't be afraid of us. We mean you no harm. "

Taylor sat in silent terror as she tried to absorb what she had just heard. Somewhere close by was a spirit of a creature. This was something she thought existed only in legends and ghost stories. More important was that this spirit was speaking to her kindly, as if she were a friend. For a wild second, Taylor wanted to scream for her mother and banish the spirits, but curiosity won over fear.

Instead of screaming, she asked, "Where did you come from? I mean, spirits are supposed to be nasty things that lurk around graveyards and abandoned places. But you don't seem nasty at all, and we certainly aren't in a graveyard."

Her question was followed by a momentary silence before the soft voice filled the air again.

"We live in a parallel dimension to your world. You probably don't know this, but there are an infinite number of solar systems in the universe. Every year, the universe expands more and more and new solar systems are made. For example, I lived on a planet that circled around two suns. Its system is close to your own. Now that I am a spirit, I can journey to any dimension, galaxy, or planet. Spirits live within people. We can live even within a newborn child. In exchange for providing us a place to live, we protect the person. When the person dies, we return to the parallel dimension until we choose a new home. We are immortal creatures.

"When humans sleep, the spirit can travel wherever it pleases, but when the person awakens, the spirit returns. The human brain sends special impulses that we use to find our way back to our person. Each human has a unique impulse frequency, meaning that no two impulses are the same. When a person dies, the brain stops sending impulses, which lets us know we cannot return to the body."

Suddenly, the voice paused and grew very quiet. "You should be resting. We have talked enough for today. Perhaps we can speak again another time."

"Please, please wait!" Taylor pleaded. "I've never heard you speak before, and I want to know why my mother can't hear you."

"The average person cannot hear us," the voice replied. "Only those who have, as you humans say, 'turned on' a certain portion of your mind can hear us. Humans do not usually use this area of your brain. When you fell, the blow to your head must have affected this part so now you can hear us."

"Wow!" Taylor breathed softly. As she listened to the soft patter of footsteps outside in the hallway, she thought of another question to ask. "Is this the same part of the brain that allows some people to have psychic powers?"

"Indeed. When this part is activated, it allows some people to see visions of the future or contact the dead. For others, it grants telekinetic powers. But not all people enjoy this gift. I am not certain that you will like it. I can get rid of your powers if you do not want to hear us. I can change your mind back to the way it was."

"No! Of course I want to hear you!" Taylor cried. "I'm very interested in you! Please, tell me more!"

"Very well, but not right now. You must rest, and I have things that must be attended to." Then, the voice changed. It became softer and stranger than before. Taylor heard only three words after the change.

"Sleep, sleep, sleep . . ."

Chapter Six

Taylor felt her eyelids lower with fatigue. She began to fall . . .

Taylor gazed at the retreating rider. It felt good to know there would be a place to rest ahead. How many countless villages did the refugees have to bypass? Even the churches that were supposed to care for the poor and hungry refused to let them in. Many cities had closed their gates to all but their own residents. Soldiers patrolled outside the gates. They had been warned that if they let anyone inside, then not only would they be hanged, but their families with them.

But the Black Plague spread faster than the wind could blow. Doctors were helpless and unable to relieve those who had contracted the disease. There was no cure for the terrible disease, although some very lucky people had managed to survive. No one knew the source of the disease, and therefore, no one could find a cure. People died in their homes, on the plains, and in the forests. Houses stood empty. There was no one to take care of gardens or plants anymore, so they grew wild and untamed. Entire castles were empty of life. There was no sign whether the people had fled or simply died. Everything was in ruins.

Soon, the roar of ocean waves reached Taylor's ears. Somewhere close by, she heard the hissing of sea spray and the crashing of water upon land. She ran ahead of the other villagers and over a hill that lay before them. Throwing herself over the peak, she caught sight of the sea for the first time. Taylor had heard countless stories of the great waters that covered the world in her village, but never had she laid eyes upon their magnificent beauty. Her eyes glowed with a flaming light and her mouth formed unknown words.

"Taylor!" Sarah called from behind, "come this way. The castle is ahead."

With a final sigh of joy, Taylor tore down the hill again and joined her parents. In her heart, she promised herself that she would visit the sea again soon.

Taylor and the other villagers approached the castle. Near the gates, she saw Erik giving orders to the soldiers who guarded the gates and walls. The castle was old and covered with moss and ivy that dangled from the walls and windows. When the villagers approached, they were quickly let inside.

Taylor gasped in awe of the castle grounds. Great flowered bushes lined the walkway all the way to the castle. A steady stream flowed through the gardens, giving the plants life and beauty. Blossoming trees gazed over the bushes at the weary travelers, waving their long branches as if urging them to safety.

You are quite lucky, Taylor thought to the plants. *You have no need to fear this dreadful disease.*

Even greater than the garden was the view of the ocean, for the great sea spread endlessly beyond the castle walls. Now, Taylor could gaze at its marvels every day.

Finally, the villagers passed through the castle doors and into the reception chamber. A blast of heat erupted in Taylor's face. An enormous fireplace, resembling a giant oven, burned before them. She saw food lying deep within the flames that blasted from the fireplace. Above the fire, suspended by thick chains, hung a cauldron, from which came the smell of a delicious stew. The smell made Taylor dizzy and suddenly weak. She had barely eaten for quite some time. The light in her eyes faded.

Someone's powerful hands grabbed her before she fell and carried her over to the vast table that had been placed in the hall for the villagers. Taylor sat down upon a wooden bench.

"Thank you," she whispered. Then, she looked up and blushed crimson. Erik stood beside her.

"Eat and rest well. Your room has already been prepared," he told her before moving on to the next villagers.

Soon, Erik's soldiers brought a little stew in a large, clay pot. "It is very dangerous to eat a lot at once after a long hunger," they warned.

The villagers pounced on the food at once. Soon everyone sat at the table full, satisfied, and content, their eyelids lowered from exhaustion. Taylor glanced over at

Amanda. The girl was already asleep and using their mother, Sarah, as a pillow.

Lucky girl, Taylor thought. *You should be glad they let you ride in the carriage instead of walking with the rest of us.*

Taylor glanced around as she noticed a lady dressed in a black and white dress approach.

"I am one of the count's maids. I was ordered to take you to your room," she said.

"Thank you," Taylor replied.

Alex picked up the sleeping Amanda and the family followed the maid to the opposite side of the hall. There, another vast room awaited them. A large bed stood in the center of the room. It was covered with beautifully woven sheets and pillows. Next to the bed, on a floor that was covered with the skins of a great variety of animals, lay thick covers.

"Rest well, everyone," the maid called, lighting a few candles before she left.

Sarah and Amanda lay down upon the bed. Alex and Taylor chose the most comfortable spots on the floor. As soon as Taylor's head touched the pillow, she fell into a deep sleep.

Chapter Seven

"Good morning, my dear," Sarah whispered, bending over Taylor. "I have very good news. The doctor has given me permission to take you home! I've already called Alex. He'll pick us up in half an hour. Shall we get you ready to leave this place?"

Taylor was startled by someone knocking on the door. A nurse walked in, carrying a tray of food. She suddenly remembered how long it had been since she had last eaten, and her mouth watered at the prospect of a good meal. Behind the nurse came another young lady with a stack of papers for Sarah to sign.

"So, how do you feel?" the nurse asked kindly.

"Great!" Taylor replied. "I'm so glad to finally go home!"

An entire hour had passed since Sarah began watching Taylor. Taylor sat at the kitchen table, gazing ceaselessly at the blue sky through a window. Sarah sadly realized that she would never again see her child completely relaxed and at peace with the world. Taylor was quite motionless now. Her hair fluttered over her forehead, her eyebrows were furrowed, and she was deep in thought.

Almost one year had passed since Taylor had left the hospital. All this time, she had tried her very hardest to keep to herself. Sometimes, Sarah heard her talking to herself when she locked herself into her room. Sarah had discussed her daughter's seclusion with various doctors many times. They all attempted to calm her by telling her that it would all pass in due time.

Since her fall into the garage, Taylor had graduated middle school and finished writing her novel, which was published in April. In July, a local Barnes and Nobles bookstore invited her to do a book signing. She read parts of her book aloud to the children who gathered in the store that day and answered their questions.

Taylor was overjoyed at the bookstore, but when she returned home, her eyes dimmed, and her smile quickly faded. Taylor played with Amanda only when Sarah forced her to, and even then for only brief periods of time. In the evenings, Taylor walked outside with Don and, occasionally, met up with Erik. The young man visited her at her home a few times and had even gotten to know her parents.

It was evening and time for Don's walk. Taylor hooked the leash onto the dog's collar. A year had turned Don into a full-grown dog. When he romped in the grass,

Taylor no longer had to help him climb out again. He could now visit Taylor in her room upstairs whenever he liked. Don bounded happily up the street, barking with glee. Taylor laughed at his playfulness. Suddenly, she noticed Erik running up the street toward her.

"Hey! How's it going?" he asked with his ever-present grin.

"All right," she sighed.

"What do you mean 'all right'? You can't be all right when you sound that sad." He finally caught up with her and slowed down to match her stride.

Taylor walked in silence for some time. Then, she stopped and turned to look at Erik. "If you really want to know why I'm so sad, I'll tell you."

"Yes, I really want to know what's wrong. I'd like to help, if I can."

"I don't even know where to begin," Taylor sighed again. "Do you remember when I fell from the second floor into the garage last year?"

"Of course."

"Well, since then I've been having these strange dreams about the past. It's almost as if we all lived many centuries ago. On rare occasions, I even see the present and very near future in my dreams. For example, last night I dreamed about going outside to walk Don. I saw you come up to me on your daily run and ask me what was wrong just like tonight," Taylor said, reddening deeply.

"So, I guess that means you were waiting for me, huh?" Erik asked.

"Yeah," Taylor replied.

Erik stared at his young friend. His eyes filled with amazement and fear. Taylor smiled back at him, misreading his expression. Then, Erik explained his shock.

"I've been having strange dreams too. But my dreams are of the future, not of the past!" Eric chuckled and said, "In fact, I recently dreamed you and I stole some ancient jewelry together."

They heard a dog barking softly in the distance. The wind around them picked up slightly, and an intense chill surrounded Taylor for a moment, but in the next second, it was gone.

Erik gazed at Taylor again, but this time without a shadow of a smile on his face.

"What do you think it all means?" he asked.

Taylor paused, looking first at the ground and then at Erik. "I don't know. I just know this is all very mysterious. But right now, I have to get going. My parents are expecting me."

Without waiting for a response, she turned around and ran home.

Taylor's heart was thumping wildly. Speaking to no one in particular, she breathed, "What's going on? Why is all this happening?" Slowly, the reality of what Erik had said started to reach her. *Then I'm not the only one with strange dreams,* she thought. *Oh, how I wish the spirits would speak to me again. I bet they would know what to do. Perhaps they could even explain what's going on.*

When Taylor returned to her room, she tried desperately to call the spirits for advice. Lying on her bed, the many questions she wanted the voices to answer rushed through her head. But the only reply she received was silence.

Rolling over on her side, she looked out the window at the darkening sky. Her eyes searched the stars, looking for an answer to the mysterious puzzle surrounding her. Her mind was filled with thoughts of her dreams, the spirits, and Erik's words, but the darkness from outside soon crept into her mind, and she quickly fell asleep.

Chapter Eight

Taylor awakened at the sound of a creaking door. She stood up, smoothed out the folds in her dress, brushed her long hair with her fingers, and walked quietly through the door, taking care not to awaken the rest of her family. She entered the great chamber where the fireplace still burned brightly, warming the room. Rows of torches lined the walls, alive and blazing with flames. On the floor beneath the torches lay villagers, wrapped snugly in thick, feathered blankets.

Taylor treaded cautiously through the castle, making sure she did not disturb anyone with her dress. There was utter silence in the castle, broken only by the crackling of the logs in the fireplace. When Taylor approached the entrance to the chamber, she heard unidentifiable voices speaking outside. Taylor opened the heavy wooden door to peer at the people on the other side. Erik and his parents stood outside in the garden, along with several women. They appeared to be examining a carriage that was parked there. The countess, Erik's mother, was begging the count to allow someone to be brought up to her room.

"But she's already ill," the count said. "What good will it do to risk infecting us?"

"Don't worry. I can manage it," the countess replied.

Taylor examined the countess. She was a very beautiful woman, but there were dark circles under her eyes from many sleepless nights. She wore a stunning green velvet dress, a necklace with one enormous emerald, and earrings and a bracelet that matched the necklace.

One of the ladies walked over to the carriage and picked up a small child that looked to be no older than five. With the child in her hands, the lady walked across the garden and up the steps to the castle. The child wailed pitifully. When the lady passed close to Taylor, the girl peeked around the door again and caught a glimpse of the child. The little girl was covered with dark spots. The countess followed the lady, her hands folded together in prayer. The procession continued to the countess' bedchamber, where the girl was placed onto the bed. Just then, the countess noticed Taylor, who had followed them.

"Would you like to help me?" she asked, smiling warmly.

"Yes, I'd be delighted to help in any way I can," Taylor replied.

"Very well, then. Everyone, please go to your rooms and rest. My new helper will remain here with me," the countess announced. When they had all left and the door was closed, she turned to Taylor and said, "You are not afraid, are you?"

"I don't think so," Taylor whispered.

"Know that there is no reason to worry. We shall not get sick. You see, the emerald stones in my jewelry are very special stones," the countess explained. "These emeralds have been handed down in my family from generation to generation. These emeralds can rid a person of the Black Plague or any other disease. But if anyone outside our bloodline uses them, they can only use them once to heal. After that, the stones will bring disease and a curse upon them. If I place the necklace upon this girl's forehead, she shall be cured. In order to be safe from the disease, you must wear something that has the magical stones in it as well."

The countess handed Taylor the sparkling bracelet. She pulled it on and looked up for further instructions.

"Now, take the girl by one hand. I shall take her other hand, and then we will pray together." Taylor noticed that the moment the countess began praying, a tiny spark burned brightly inside the emerald stone . . .

Chapter Nine

Fresh air poured from the open window into Taylor's room. She awoke at once and thought, *We really don't know much about our past. I can never allow something like what happened before happen to mankind again.* Strange, she suddenly realized. *I dreamed of the countess' emerald necklace, and Erik had a dream about the two of us stealing an ancient piece of jewelry. This can't be a coincidence. After all, there is a very fine line between coincidence and fate, and I'm afraid we've crossed it.*

Behind the door, Taylor heard a deep sniffing sound. Don, realizing that his owner was awake, decided to let her know he was waiting for her. Taylor stood up and let him inside. Don started to jump, licking her hands at the height of each bounce.

"Yes, I know. You want to be walked. Well, just give me a minute and we'll go outside!" Taylor said.

Taylor ran into the bathroom and combed her hair and brushed her teeth. Then, she scooped the terrier into her hands and ran down the stairs. The leash was already waiting for them by the door. Taylor clipped the leash onto Don's collar, and they went outside.

The wind blew at her back, urging her to go faster. She felt almost as if she could fly off into the sky. The scent of blooming flowers reached her nose. She inhaled deeply, wanting to smell every one of them.

Suddenly, Taylor heard Erik's now familiar voice. "Hello, princess. Sleep well?"

"All right, I guess," she said. But in her mind, a silent war was raging. She was torn between two choices. *Should I tell Erik about the dream I had last night, or should I keep quiet?* In the end, Taylor decided that until she figured out what her dream was about and whether or not it really had anything to do with Erik's dream, she would not reveal what she had seen. If this was truly not a coincidence, things could get very dangerous very quickly.

"Now, this might sound strange to you, but last night I was watching the news and I saw the exact same jewelry that I saw in my dreams. It's on display at an exhibit!" Erik cried.

"Where's the exhibit? Can we go see it?"

"It's downtown. The jewelry is actually in someone's house, so I guess you could call it a private exhibit. If you want," Erik added quietly, "we could go there together."

Taylor felt her heart beating hard against her chest. Swallowing hard to rid herself of the strange sensation, she said, "I'd love to go! But first, I have to ask my parents. They wouldn't like it very much if I just left without a word. Actually . . . how about we meet at my house in . . . oh say . . . two hours. How does that sound?"

"Perfect!" Erik replied, and waved goodbye as he turned to leave. Taylor smiled brightly at him, waved her adieu as well, and returned home as fast as she could walk.

When she arrived home, Taylor grabbed a rag to do a bit of cleaning to surprise her parents and put them in a good mood. She ran the cloth over all the furniture to dust it and opened all the windows wide to let the early sunlight in. When the rooms were clean, Taylor walked to the kitchen. She took four eggs out of the refrigerator and cracked them over a skillet and put the skillet on the stove. Then, she turned the stove on and waited while the eggs sizzled and cooked. When they were fully cooked, she transferred the eggs to a nice ceramic dish and covered them with the matching lid to keep them warm. After placing the dish on the kitchen table, she also got out a box of cereal from one of the cupboards and a gallon of milk from the refrigerator and set them down next to the eggs. Taylor glanced at the food she had prepared and smiled. "Now, everything's ready!"

She then ran upstairs and took a quick shower to be ready for Erik. She reached into her closet and drew out dress after dress, trying to decide which one would look the prettiest.

"No, not that one. I don't like this one either! And that one certainly won't do! Oh, this dress is perfect!" she said, picking out a green silk dress that was hidden behind all of the others. It was her very favorite. Taylor then ran to her bathroom. *The perfume Mom gave me . . . just a drop behind each ear.*

Taylor returned to the kitchen and looked at the table once again. *No, this really isn't enough.* She got out some salami from the fridge and sliced it into thin pieces. She placed them onto a plate and then added cheese and bread to make sandwiches. *Now everyone will really be in a good mood. Just what I need . . . Mom and Dad have to let me go!*

Soon, Amanda woke up and started moving around, waking everyone else up, too. It was Saturday, and so the girl awoke before the rest. Within ten minutes, the entire family was together at the table.

"Taylor, this is delicious!" Alex exclaimed. "The table looks great and the silverware spotless! But, why aren't you eating anything?"

"I'm eating, I'm eating," Taylor retorted and grabbed some cheese. After a short pause, she added, "Dad, I wanted to ask you a favor. There's an exhibit on display right now in downtown Atlanta. May I please go see it?"

"I can't take you today," he replied sadly. "I've got several appointments that will keep me busy. How about another time?"

"I can't take you either," Sarah added. "I need to take Amanda to her music lesson. How about we go tomorrow? Is it open on Sunday?"

At that moment, the ring of the doorbell sounded throughout the house. Amanda leapt off her chair and raced to open the door before anyone else had the chance. Erik stood in the doorway, smiling.

"So, the prince has arrived!" she laughed. "Step right in, your highness!" She bowed and stepped aside.

"Yes, come in, Erik. Sit down!" Sarah told him.

Erik walked over to the table and sat down in the only remaining empty chair, but refused any food, saying he had already eaten.

"Are you looking forward to school?" Alex asked Erik.

"Yes! In ten days, I'll start my last year of high school. If all goes well, I hope to get into a good college and then law school."

"Well in that case, I'd like to wish you the best of luck fulfilling your dreams!" Alex smiled at the boy. "But for now, how about ice cream for everyone!"

"No, thanks," Erik replied gently. "You know, there's a private exhibit of ancient jewelry downtown. I've arranged with the owner to view the collection at his house. Could Taylor come with me?"

"Well . . ." Alex exchanged looks with Sarah, who nodded encouragingly, "of course she can. You look like a fine, responsible young man to me. But," he turned to Taylor, "make sure you take your cell phone in case we have to call you."

"Oh, Dad, thanks!" Taylor cried, running toward the front door with Erik at her heels. "Bye! See you later!"

When they got outside, Taylor was quite taken aback by the sudden change in the weather. The brilliant blue sky that had sparkled overhead in the early morning had given way to a mass of darkness. Black clouds hung low in the sky and the streets were shrouded in shadows. Along the edges of the sidewalk, street lamps burned brightly. The few cars that drove slowly along the street all had their headlights on to illuminate the murky road.

The two friends climbed into Erik's red Honda Element. The seats were made of leather, and the car had a DVD player and a sunroof. As soon as Taylor buckled her seatbelt, Erik backed the car out of the driveway and headed toward downtown.

The entire freeway was flooded in an ocean of lights. Streetlights and car headlights blared and flashed. The dark clouds pressed down on the city, almost as if they were foreshadowing impending doom.

"Is there anything you'd like to talk to me about?" Erik suddenly threw at Taylor.

"Not really," she replied truthfully.

Erik sighed heavily and continued to pilot the car along the freeway. It was still a long way to the exhibit.

Chapter Ten

Several months before . . .

Mr. Chester had lived in his house for as long as he could remember. The house was old and ancient looking. The vast wooden door loomed over the front steps, and the yard was enclosed, surrounded with great brick walls. The steep, sloping roof was made of thick cedar. A chimney extended from the wall to the right of the door and up past the rooftop. The old house had a long history of Chesters who had lived there before.

Mr. Chester himself was not young. He had thick, curly white hair and sparkling blue eyes. His hooked nose looked almost like an eagle's beak, except for the horn-rimmed glasses perched on his nose. He walked with the aid of a beautifully carved oak cane. Mr. Chester was an old-fashioned man who had lived his entire life surrounded by antiques and old furniture.

Behind the old house was a garden. Lilies peeked out from behind their half opened petals, roses danced in the sun, and pansies gazed shyly from out of the shadows. Mr. Chester could sit for hours in his garden, admiring all the living things and watching the clouds race to pile on top of each other.

But the thing he loved most about his garden was an ancient oak that stood at its very center. The oak was charred and black. Mr. Chester gazed upon it, remembering the story his father had once told him. A long time ago, a bolt of lightning had struck the tree, causing it to burst into flames. One of his relatives, who was standing under the tree, had died when a flaming branch broke off and pinned him to the ground. However, the tree did not fall. The strong roots of the oak anchored it safely to the ground.

Many years had passed since that fateful storm. The remaining branches of the tree were now dying. Parts of the bark had chipped off. The condition of the oak seemed to foretell tragic events yet to come and served as a reminder of those in the past. Still, Mr. Chester loved the old tree. He grew up with the oak and loved it like a dear friend. And yet, he also knew that leaving the tree in such a state was dangerous. So Mr. Chester had finally decided to have it removed. Today, he would say his final farewell to his old friend.

Resolving himself to the final parting he would have to make with the tree, Mr. Chester returned to the garden. *Forgive me, my dearest friend.* He gazed up at the old tree and sighed. *Never again will you have green leaves to brighten your bark or acorns to weigh down your branches. Birds will no longer weave their nests in your boughs. Squirrels will never again hide your acorns in their homes. The time of joy and love has passed not only for you, but for me as well, my beloved friend.* The old gentleman approached the tree and wrapped his arms around the tree as far as he could. The trunk was far too thick for anyone to reach all the way around. *Farewell, my friend, farewell!*

At that moment, the doorbell rang. Mr. Chester let go of the tree sadly and went to open the door. As promised, the tree removal company was there right on time. Before he let the men go to their duties, he asked them to tear up the roots and cart away the tree without his being present. It would be too sad to witness the death of his beloved friend. He gave them his cell phone number and instructed the company to call him when the deed was done. With one last somber look at the tree, he left the house and went to a local park.

A great deal of time passed after Mr. Chester said his goodbye. All the tears had dried on his face. He looked up at the clouds floating overhead, although he didn't really pay too much attention to them. The park around him was quite beautiful, but it was not really the best time to go for a stroll. Sadness dwelt in his heart. Still, sitting in the park made the old man feel better. It was better than sitting in some café.

Suddenly, Mr. Chester felt a cold wetness wash over his foot. He looked down and saw that he had stepped into the river that he had been walking alongside. Mr. Chester shook off the water and looked out at the river.

Large boulders jutted out from the center of the river, making excellent perches for many ducks and geese. Some of the ducks screeched loudly at each other, bristling their feathers and flapping their wings.

Strange, Mr. Chester thought as he walked along the riverbank. *I wonder why the company hasn't called me yet? Surely they've had enough time to remove one tree by now. Maybe they forgot to call.* He continued to walk along the riverbank, vaguely enjoying the trees and birds, until his cell phone finally rang. Mr. Chester jumped in surprise, but he recovered quickly, pulled out the phone, and answered the call.

"Please, come home as soon as you can," the man on the other end of the line gasped. "There's something here you need to see."

Mr. Chester reached the edge of the park as quickly as his elderly legs would carry him and hailed a taxi. The taxi pulled up to the curb, and in minutes, he was back home. His mind was so filled with questions and anticipation that he hardly noticed the ride. Mr. Chester threw the driver some money from his wallet and rushed into his house and on to the backyard. One of the workers from the tree removal company met him by the door. As they walked, the worker said, "Mr. Chester, I'm sorry this is taking so long, but we were forced to stop because we found something hidden underneath your oak's roots."

The old man nodded to the worker, his eyes full of interest and excitement. Wondering what had been concealed for so many years beneath his tree, Mr. Chester followed the younger man to the garden, where the oak lay sadly on its side. He felt a twinge of sadness in his heart as he cast a weary eye over the tree, but he quickly

turned his head away. There was no time for tears now. The two men approached the edge of the hole where the tree's roots had been. Mr. Chester peered over the edge and gasped at what he saw.

Lying at the bottom of the ditch, half covered by earth and old leaves, was an ancient, rusty chest. Three of the workers quickly pulled the chest out of the hole and placed it beside the oak. Mr. Chester knelt beside the chest and brushed off the dirt and mud that was caked on the old thing. He was anxious to open it and find out what secrets it carried within. However, the chest was shut tight with a heavy iron lock. Luckily, the lock was so old and rusty that a good hard strike with a shovel from one of the young men was enough to crack it open. With trembling hands, Mr. Chester opened the lid and gazed inside.

At first, the entire treasure appeared to be a bunch of matted, torn dresses and other old garments. But when Mr. Chester reached inside to pull out the clothes, his fingertips brushed against something very hard. He took one of the dresses and unwrapped it carefully. Inside were a golden bracelet and a pair of shiny gold earrings. Another ragged shirt had a silvery cup hidden inside. A pair of mud-caked pants contained a pair of rubies. But the most amazing object was hidden in the last gown at the very bottom of the chest. Wrapped tightly inside the flowing green material was a necklace of divine beauty. The chain was made of white gold that sparkled like the sun. Yet, what attracted Mr. Chester's eye more than anything else was the enormous emerald stone set into the center of the necklace.

Chapter Eleven

Taylor and Erik drove up to the old house and parked the car in the driveway. The two young people got out of the car and walked slowly up to the ancient wooden door. Taylor reached for the doorbell, exchanged a look with her friend, and pressed the button. A booming ring echoed throughout the house. She instinctively stepped back and grabbed Erik's hand. He smiled gently at her, and then they both turned to stare at the door.

A tall woman of about twenty-five opened the door. She had a warm, sweet smile, shiny hazel eyes, and reddish hair. A black dress stretched over her curving form, complete with a brilliant pearl necklace around her neck. She smiled kindly at the two teens and said, "Come in and sit right down. Mr. Chester will see you in just a moment."

Taylor stepped through the doorway and took a second to examine her surroundings. They were in the living room. She walked across the room and sank down onto the sofa among the many pillows that lay there. The old, worn leather pillows were soft and warm to the touch. Taylor's feet rested comfortably on the plush rug that stretched across the floor. She looked up at one of the pictures on the wall and recognized it as one by Salvador Dali. The picture was like the one she saw in a museum in Florida. There were three faces in the drawing, one representing a baby, another a middle-aged man, and the last an old man. Unlike the one in the museum, this one had the silhouette of a young woman beside the middle-aged man. In fact, Taylor had never even seen this exact picture in any book about Dali's art. *How strange . . .*

She tore her gaze away from the picture and looked up at the old fireplace set into a third wall. On the mantel was a photograph that, from the faded colors, seemed to have been taken years ago. It showed an old man and a teenage boy standing together happily under an enormous oak tree. The oak tree, it seemed, had suffered some sort of mishap. It was charred and looked like it had been through a large fire.

Just then, the doorbell rang again, and the red-haired lady opened the door to allow several more people to enter the house. "Please have a seat in here. Mr. Chester will be with you in just a moment," Taylor heard the woman say again. Seven people walked into the room and spread to various locations. One of the ladies sat on the sofa beside Taylor. Two other ladies settled on two wooden chairs in a corner across the room from Taylor and engaged in a private conversation. The last visitors, four men, also talking among themselves, stood in the center of the room.

At long last, the old gentleman appeared in the doorway. He looked around at all his guests and smiled.

"Good day to you all," he said. The two women in the corner abruptly ended their conversation and looked up at the newcomer. He nodded at them before continuing.

"My name is Robert Chester. I'm very happy to welcome all of you to my home." Mr. Chester then described how he made the strange discovery of the chest underneath the old oak and promised to show them the pride and joy of the collection. He motioned with his hand for them to follow him to the exhibit.

Taylor lagged slightly behind the other guests. She tried to focus on the house and the beautiful collection of antiques, but her thoughts kept drifting elsewhere. Something was oddly familiar about the furnishings, but she simply couldn't put her finger on what it was.

"Isn't all this stuff amazing?" Erik asked her as they gazed down at a display case containing a golden bracelet and a pair of shiny gold earrings.

"It sure is," Taylor said. Erik nodded and they continued to the next display case.

Finally, Taylor approached the display at the far end of the room. There was an air of importance around this item, for Mr. Chester had not left the stand since everyone entered the room. All of the other people crowded around whatever was beneath the glass, uttering sounds of excitement. Taylor waited until the crowd had drifted to other parts of the exhibit before approaching the last item. As she caught a glimpse of the jewelry shining behind the glass, Taylor's heart thumped painfully in her chest. She heard an odd ringing sound in her head and ceased to think at all. For just one moment, it seemed as if she was once again falling through darkness.

"Don't turn around," Taylor heard a very strange voice say. It echoed mysteriously all around her and made her feel as if she was inside a cave. She realized there was nobody on Earth who spoke in that manner. The spirit had finally decided to talk to her again. "Don't say anything aloud," the spirit continued. "I can read your every thought."

I've called to you so many times. Why haven't you talked to me for such a long time? Taylor asked the spirit in thought. *Why have you chosen to speak now? So many strange things have happened that I don't understand . . .*

"Taylor, it is difficult for humans to understand our world while living in yours. I thought our getting to know each other would only confuse you and complicate your life. I decided it was in your best interest for us not to talk. It has hurt me not to answer you, but I thought it was best. Besides, I'm very sorry that I forgot to mention it earlier, but we can go only to homes where someone had already died. Because you live in a brand new house, there is no trace of the dead there. We go to homes where people passed away and to hospitals where countless souls have parted with their bodies. Even if I thought that answering you was the right thing to do, speaking with you would have been impossible."

I thought that you'd forgotten me or were angry with me for some reason and had decided to never speak to me again. But why have you chosen to speak now?

Taylor looked at the necklace with the single emerald stone behind the display glass and felt her heart thump even harder.

"Taylor, I know your dreams. Yes, that is what you believe it to be. That necklace belonged to the countess. In her hands, it returned life to those who where hopelessly condemned to death by the Black Plague. But that necklace can save lives only if it is used with the countess' complete set of jewelry."

The emerald bracelet and the earrings!

"Yes. Only when all three items are worn together and the ancient prayer is spoken over them will the emeralds heal. But, there is more to the countess' jewelry than meets the eye. When the necklace was placed upon the head of someone who was ill, it absorbed the evil of the disease. If it is worn without the bracelet and the earrings, it will bring disease to the person who wears it. The earrings, if worn alone, are quite dangerous as well, although they aren't nearly as deadly as the necklace. The earrings also bring disease to whoever wears them."

What about the bracelet? What evil does it do?

"The bracelet does no evil at all. It brings only good luck and joy to its owner. As long as the bracelet is upon your arm, you are safe from all diseases and will have great luck."

But that means, Taylor realized excitedly, *that if I can get all three pieces of jewelry, then I can save the lives of all those who are ill or near death, just like the countess did!*

"Sadly, that's not possible. You are forgetting only the countess' descendants can save many lives. Even if you acquire the entire set, you may save only one life. After that, the jewelry will be useless to you. If the set is not kept together, then the individual pieces must be hidden for the safety of others. That is why they were hidden in the chest under the oak all these years. They were never meant to be found."

But what can I do then? Taylor asked desperately. But no matter how hard she pleaded this last question, the spirit did not answer.

"What did you find that's so interesting?" Erik walked over to where Taylor was standing, looking puzzled. When he approached the final display case, he gasped when he saw the necklace.

"But this is . . . "

Taylor placed her hand over his and whispered gently, "I know. This is the necklace from our dreams."

Taylor grabbed Erik by the hand and pulled him toward the door. They quickly thanked Mr. Chester and hurried out. Erik remained silent and thoughtful throughout the entire drive home, his eyes glazed over. Taylor, however, talked without as much as a single pause. She told Erik everything that had happened to her since her fall. She told him about the spirits, her strange dreams, the Black Plague, the countess, and the enchanted jewelry that had the power to cure any disease.

At long last, Taylor was quiet. After a long silence, Erik finally came to his senses. "Don't worry about the necklace. That old Mr. Chester has it guarded under lock and key. As long as it remains in his house under that glass, I don't think that there's any way it could harm anyone. After all," he paused for a moment, his eyes darting about nervously, "no one is going to steal it, right?"

Taylor only smiled at him and said nothing.

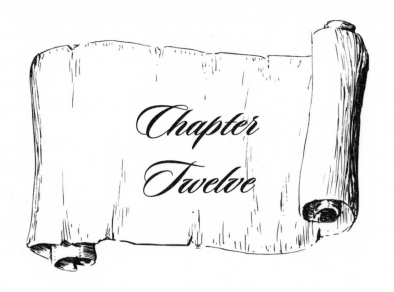

Chapter Twelve

What a joy it was to return to those carefree days when life was just an extended school schedule and nothing could possibly go wrong. The days were back when children could play and learn together in school without any worries, except when the occasional test came up, and they had to study hard. But other than that, life was simple and easy when school began. Taylor stood at the bus stop, waiting impatiently for the big, yellow bus to arrive. Today was the very first day of the new school year. She was excited to find out who her new classmates would be this year. She was not worried in the least about her classes because she had always enjoyed learning.

The other kids in Taylor's class had heard that the author of *The Galaxy Watch* would be learning alongside them. They argued and pushed to get seats close to her. It seemed that everywhere she went, students mobbed her with questions about her book. Most children her age disliked reading, but they seemed fascinated by the fact

that she had actually written a book. They loved asking how she managed to get her book published and how much money she made.

Some stared at Taylor as if she were some kind of alien. For the girls, the most important things in life were going to the mall, hanging out, talking with cute guys, and buying the latest clothes. The boys enjoyed playing football and video games. They counted the minutes until school ended, eager to hang out in the video arcade at the mall. Taking the time to actually do something useful never crossed their minds.

But now, even Taylor counted every passing second. She did not enjoy all of the attention she was getting, and was quite anxious to be rid of it all. Even during lunch, many kids from various grades came up to her asking if it was true that she had written and illustrated a book. To top it all off, someone's mother walked up to her and told her that her daughter, who was in elementary school, wanted Taylor to make a presentation for her class.

But Taylor also had her own problems to worry about, aside from the newfound popularity. Because she had moved from another school system, she had to retake a placement test to qualify for the gifted program. She also had to take forms to each of the teachers in the gifted program and ask them if they would consider her for their classes and allow her to take the necessary exams. Between locating the different teachers and persuading them to sign the necessary papers, Taylor had to answer what seemed like hundreds of questions about her novel and the various happenings in her life. All in all, the start of the school year was difficult—not in terms of learning, but in finding time to learn.

At last, the school day ended, and Taylor boarded the bus that would take her home. She looked around expectantly at all the smiling and joking faces, but there was one face that she did not spot. Erik was not on the bus, nor did she recall seeing him in school. *Perhaps he drove to school,* she wondered, *but I still should have seen him around somewhere.*

As soon as Taylor walked up the sidewalk to her house, Sarah pulled open the door and urged her daughter inside. "What's going on, Mom?"

"Your aunt and uncle are coming from Detroit for a visit!" she said quickly as she shoved a duster into Taylor's hands. "You have to help me clean the house. Your dad is already taking the car to the car wash. Amanda went with him. Now, come on, come on! There's no time to lose!"

The entire house was organized and spotless by the time Sarah and Taylor were finished. From the moment Taylor had come from school, they had been busy sweeping, dusting, cooking, and cleaning the house from top to bottom. Every doorknob was sparkling in the glow of gleaming lamps hanging from the ceiling. Their glow also reflected off the shiny hardwood floors throughout the house. At ten in the evening, the doorbell finally gave a long, high-pitched dong.

"They're here!" Sarah cried, rushing to the door, tripping over a new rug along the way.

She hastily rearranged her shirt and flung open the door, revealing three people standing in the doorway—a lovely lady, a short, rather plump man, and a young man around the age of eighteen. Taylor's aunt immediately threw her arms around Sarah's neck, planting a kiss on her cheek. "Oh Sarah, I'm so glad to see you again!" she said. "And what a gorgeous house!"

Sarah's sister looked over her shoulder, eyeing the house eagerly.

"Everyone, please come say hello to Vicky," Sarah managed to gasp through her sister's strangling hug. "Michael," she motioned to the fat man, who nodded, and finally to the young man, "and . . ."

"Kyle!" Amanda cried eagerly, rushing up to her older cousin and hugging him round the middle. "Yay! Come on, let me show you the playroom!"

The youngster clutched Kyle's hand in hers and pulled him along behind her. With a desperate, pleading look at everyone, Kyle reluctantly followed Amanda to the playroom.

Everyone exchanged hugs and greetings. A warm, lively conversation ensued as the group moved from the foyer to the living room. Michael sat down on a sofa, chuckling merrily at a joke Alex had just told him. Sarah directed the newcomers upstairs and instructed them to pick out guest rooms that suited them and to freshen up for dinner. Vicky was the first to head upstairs, eager to change into one of her brand new outfits. Michael waved off the offer and remained in the living room with Alex.

When Sarah and Vicky reached the second floor, they stopped by the playroom and suggested that Amanda release Kyle so he could get ready for dinner. Kyle smiled weakly and quickly followed his mother and aunt to the nearest guest room.

When Vicky and Kyle came downstairs, the two families sat down at the kitchen table. Vicky smoothed out her bright red dress and turned to talk to Sarah. Kyle chose a seat across the table from Amanda in fear of being forced to play with her again, but found he was quite safe from any games. Both Amanda and Taylor were so exhausted that their eyelids sagged low and their heads drooped. Taylor soon asked if they could be excused. Kyle saw this as the perfect opportunity to ask if he could play video games on his uncle's computer. Taylor and Amanda told everyone goodnight and quickly slipped away from the table while the adults chatted. The two girls bid each other good night and went quietly to their rooms.

The festivities continued late into the night. Sarah played a concert on her grand piano, Alex sang some of his favorite songs while strumming on his guitar, and Vicky and Michael recited a few poems they had written. Kyle had even joined them in their fun. In fact, they might have sung, danced, and laughed until morning if Kyle had not fallen asleep on the living room floor. Alex shook his head at the young man and told him to go off to bed.

Very soon, the entire house was filled with snores as a deep peace fell upon the home. Night had spread a blanket of comfort over the world.

Everyone was well rested and content the next morning. Jokes were told over breakfast, smiles were exchanged, and happiness surrounded them. But one person sat quietly in a corner, away from all of the joy. Taylor ignored everyone's calls and removed herself from the joy, looking worried, thoughtful, and sad. Kyle noticed her distant look and tried to cheer her up, but no matter what joke he told or how hard he attempted to make her laugh, she just sat there looking far away as if he was not even there. Finally, Kyle shrugged, returned to his parents, and busied himself with telling a story. The adults laughed and Amanda screamed with glee, hanging from Kyle's arm. Still, Taylor sat quietly in her corner.

Dark things were stirring deep in Taylor's mind. Her dreams whirled around her in a tangled web. She knew there was a connection between them, but no matter how hard she tried, she came up empty handed. There was an important link from the past to the present that she could not find. She knew it was important because the more she thought about it, the more she realized her dreams were more than just dreams after all. They had crossed the boundary between coincidence and fate.

Chapter Thirteen

At last, the first week of school was over. It had been an interesting experience, especially "Freshman Friday." Taylor had heard terrible stories from other students about the pranks that were traditionally played on new freshman as a baptism into high school. One boy was actually locked in the janitor's closet for two hours by a couple of seniors. Freshman had run screaming through the hallways as the upperclassmen chased them. Taylor managed to stay out of trouble by sticking close to groups of older students. All in all, the entire day was chaotic and crazy, and Taylor was glad it was over.

The thing that still worried Taylor most was she hadn't seen Erik anywhere. Every time she walked home from the bus, she stopped in front of Erik's door and rang the doorbell, but never got an answer. She peered through the windows, but there was no sign of life in the house. When she got home, she even called Erik and left messages on the family's answering machine, but her calls had gone unreturned.

Luckily, there was one change for the better. Since Amanda now had Kyle to play with, Taylor wasn't as burdened with her babysitting duties. She was also free from helping with the cooking because Aunt Vicky had willingly taken over that chore. The only thing she had to do was walk Don three times a day, which she was eager to do because it might give her a glimpse of Erik.

On Saturday evening, Sarah, Vicky, and Taylor cooked a splendid meal consisting of everyone's favorite foods. The entire house was filled with a warm, pleasant aroma. Soon, everyone was gathered at the table, forks and knives in hand and ready to dig into the food.

"So," Alex began, motioning towards Michael, "what've you decided about Atlanta? Do you like it here?"

Michael gave a laugh. "Like it? We love it! In fact, we've decided to move here permanently!"

Sarah gave Vicky a tight hug and whispered, "We'll finally be together again!"

Vicky jerked her head, her eyes grew wide, and she gasped for breath. Everyone around the table laughed as Sarah muttered an apology.

"If you can help us find jobs," Michael continued, "then we can buy a house somewhere around here and sell our house in Detroit."

Alex waved away the question. "Of course I can help you find a job! Why don't you go to the store with me tomorrow and see if you like my work. If so, you can work for me." He turned to Vicky and said, "And you can be my secretary. I've been looking for someone reliable, and I can really use the help. And Kyle can train to work in my company too!"

Vicky's face suddenly filled with worry. "But how will we find a house? Do you know a realtor who could help us?"

Sarah laughed and patted her sister's shoulder gently. "Not to worry. There are plenty of gorgeous houses here. I know you will find one that you will love. As for a realtor, we don't need to know one. We can pick up some real estate magazines and look at the listings. They will have the agent's name and number in the listing."

She motioned to Taylor, who looked up from her plate to listen to her mother. "Taylor, be a dear and fetch the real estate magazines from the garage. They are sitting on the shelf above the trash cans."

Turning again to Vicky, Sarah smiled excitedly and said, "I knew there was a reason I hadn't been able to throw them away."

With the magazines spread all over the kitchen table, Vicky leafed through the pages and found a few houses she wanted to see. She choose those that were closest to her sister's house. Sarah made phone calls to the realtors, and for the next few hours, the phone wasn't silent for as much as a minute. Realtors kept calling back, each trying to convince the new family that their listing was perfect.

Vicky and Sarah scheduled appointments to start viewing the houses that afternoon. Since Taylor loved looking at houses, she decided to join her mother, Michael, Vicky, and Kyle. To keep Amanda busy, Alex took her to the appliance store with him.

The first house they visited was in an area called Roswell. It was only twenty minutes from the Creekmore's home. Taylor's first impression of the subdivision was a cloning lab. All of the houses looked exactly the same. They had the same brick exterior, the same dark roof, and the same slightly sloping front lawn. However, the house they stopped in front of had an extra feature—a bright green front door instead of a white door like the other houses. Taylor smiled at the owner's bravery and wondered what they would find inside.

Taylor's joyful anticipation evaporated the moment she stepped into the foyer. The distant voices of the spirits filled the room, and she realized that some terrible tragedy must have befallen this home. Perhaps the owners were a little too brave, and not only in painting the door a color that did not match the others.

Luckily, Vicky began to feel ill as well. She quickly decided it was because of the house and shooed them out the front door.

"No, no, no! There's something wrong here. I can feel it," they heard her mutter under her breath. "Maybe the next one will be better . . ."

The next house was located in Alpharetta and only about ten minutes from the Creekmores. It was smaller than the first, but when the two families walked inside, they immediately felt at home. Everyone went to a different corner of the house to examine every detail. Taylor loved everything about it. There were three huge bedrooms, a roomy kitchen, two sets of stairs leading to the second floor—one in the foyer and the other in the kitchen. The house also included a finished basement, a formal dining room, a vast living room, and even an office. But the thing that captivated Taylor was the view from the back porch.

The house stood upon a steep hill that led down to a forest. Thick pines and oaks shot up from the ground, and the gentle chirping of birds mixed with the gurgling of a stream to create a wonderful retreat. Taylor felt herself swept away by the beauty of nature as she listened to the melody. She barely heard Vicky cry behind her, "This is my house! Michael, let's make an offer right now. I must have this house! It just feels perfect."

They went to the real estate office immediately and made an official offer on the house. It was a generous offer, and Vicky hoped that the owners would accept it. But by the time they made their offer and were ready to go home, it was nearing midnight. The silver minivan returned home under the light of a full moon. Taylor heard everyone yawn as they pulled into the driveway. Their tired feet dragged into the house as Taylor, Kyle, Michael, Vicky, and Sarah bid each other goodnight and went off to their rooms. Taylor checked on her younger sister to make sure she was safely in bed before going off to her own room.

Although she was exhausted, Taylor just couldn't sleep. She tossed and turned in bed, unable to feel even the slightest bit drowsy. *Perhaps,* she thought, *a nice warm glass of milk will help me sleep.*

She crept downstairs, silently poured herself some milk, and heated it in the microwave. When the microwave beeped to let her know the milk was ready, Taylor took the glass and sat down at the kitchen table. As she sipped her milk, her eyes roved along the walls and counters. Everything seemed to be in order. Yes, all was as it should be . . . almost.

———————————— 68 ————————————

A red light was blinking on the answering machine that sat next to the kitchen phone. Taylor walked over to the machine, pressed the button, and waited for the message to play.

The machine made a whirring sound and announced that there was one message. The caller's words sounded a bit fuzzy and made Taylor wonder where the person was calling from, but her heart flipped when she realized that it was a long awaited message from Erik.

"Hey, Taylor. This is Erik, and I'm so sorry that I worried you." The voice paused for a moment, and Taylor registered the weariness in his voice before Erik continued. "I didn't have time to call you before leaving. My family and I are in Los Angeles right now. If everything goes according to plan, we'll be back in a few days. Talk to you then. Bye!"

The machine beeped again and the kitchen lapsed into silence.

Taylor sighed sadly as she stared at the machine. Erik's message was supposed to allay her fears, not prompt more worries. His voice told her that something was terribly wrong. That night, for the very first time in her life, Taylor lay awake until morning. *Well, at least today is Sunday,* she thought as she wearily got out of bed. *I don't have to go to school, which is good because I would have certainly gotten a detention for falling asleep in class.*

Taylor decided to spend the day resting. Since reading was one of her favorite ways to relax, she got out one of her favorite books, *The Three Musketeers* by Alexandre Dumas. The story's characters came alive in her imagination, and she could see every scene as if it were happening before her. Her eyes took on a glazed expression, and she whispered aloud to no one in particular, "Ah, how beautiful their words of love sound! How bravely they risked their lives to save the honor of women!"

Her favorite character was D'Artagnan. He was brave, loyal, and always willing to stand up for what was right. However, she found D'Artagnan's enemy, the Cardinal Richelieu, to be the most intriguing character. She was impressed by his ingenious planning and the way he cleverly accomplished his goals no matter how difficult the task was. Of course, this was merely Taylor's opinion of Richelieu. The way Dumas described him, most people would take him to be a cunning and dangerous foe. The reality of the matter was Richelieu was the man behind the France many had come to know and love. Dumas had changed the world's perspective of the great man who lived his life for his country, just for the sake of a young musketeer.

Taylor put down the book and fell back onto her bed. Her mind swirled in thought. *So many things are changed for foolish reasons,* she thought sleepily. Slowly, almost unnoticeably, her breathing eased and her eyes closed. Before she knew it, she was fast asleep.

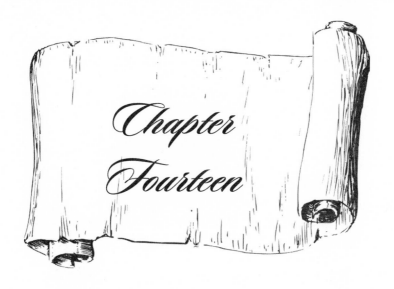

Chapter Fourteen

The sun was just setting in Los Angeles. Its final rays peeked into every building as the sun bid a last farewell before vanishing altogether. The rays fluttered faintly over the walls and floors of the many California homes, quivering gently and blending in with shadows. Even in a small clinic, lost among a tangle of other buildings, a sliver of light could be seen. The ray slipped through one of the windows in the waiting room and landed on a young man's lap.

Erik sat in the clinic, his hands and lap bathed in light, but his mind deep in darkness. *What did we do to deserve this? Why is my family being punished in this way?* His face was streaked with tears, and he trembled as he thought of the tragedy that had befallen his family. After a few moments, he stood up and began pacing the room, all the while thinking about his mother.

Erik's mother was deathly ill. She now lay almost life-less in her hospital bed, getting progressively worse by the day. Poor Erik couldn't help but wonder if she was in this condition because of him.

It all began a few months ago when his mother first complained of a pain in her leg. Erik offered to call the doctor, but his mother had point-blank refused. She told him the pain would soon pass. Erik wanted to believe her, but his instincts still told him to call the doctor. A few days later, she complained about her back. That time, he actually picked up the phone and dialed the doctor's number, but his mother wrenched it out of his hands before he could proceed any further. Shaking her head, she told him he was overreacting and to give the pain time. Nothing happened for a couple of weeks after that, so Erik calmed himself and pretended nothing was wrong. Still, his heart pounded with worry, and his inner spirit told him to call the doctor. But instead of heeding these warnings, he did nothing.

A month later, an unexpected jolt of pain shot through every nerve in his mother's body. Fortunately, Erik was with her, and she fell into his arms. In a weak and weary voice, she finally told him to call the doctor. Erik dialed the number, but his heart trembled. Somewhere deep within, he sensed it was too late.

The doctor's diagnosis allayed no one's fears. "Melanoma," he told them, one hand firm on her shoulder. "It is a terrible cancer that starts from the skin and then moves inward." His mother went to many doctors to find out where the cancer had started. Although the doctors looked over every inch of her skin, they could find nothing. The tumor was finally found in her stomach, but the metastasis had already spread all through her body. The doctors all gave the same answer, too. They all shook their heads solemnly and whispered, "It's too late to do surgery now. All we can do is try to make her comfortable by managing her pain."

Erik's father grayed before their very eyes. On the outside, he seemed to be breaking from pain in his heart, but the steely determination in his eyes said he was not giving up. Erik's father had a plan. If he had to lose his wife, he would lose her fighting. He decided to take her to a clinic in Los Angeles that specialized in experimental medications for treating cancer. He was sure that they could do something to cure his wife. But after a thorough examination and review of her medical records, even they said there was nothing they could do.

Why? Why? Erik's mind churned with this terrible question as he paced the hallway. *Why did I wait to call the doctor? I should've made the call the first day she complained. This is all my fault. A few months could have saved her life! Why?*

"Erik," his father called gently, "your mother would like to speak with you."

Erik walked toward the door in silence. His fingers felt like lead as he clutched the doorknob and entered the room. He moved slowly and dropped into a small chair near his mother's bed. Unable to contain himself any longer, he burst into tears.

His mother took his hand gently and smiled at him. In her weary voice, she said, "Don't cry. Don't cause my heart more pain than it already has to bear. What can we do but accept our fate? I so wish that I could be with you longer. If God allows, then we'll have a little more time together, but if not . . .

"There is something very important I must tell you. Erik, listen to me very carefully, for this may be the most precious thing I ever tell you. There is a very special heirloom that has been passed down in our family from generation to generation for countless years. It's a pair of ancient earrings. When my mother gave them to me, she told me to keep them safe, but to never wear them. I wanted to obey her. I really did. But one year ago I could no longer resist those beautiful earrings. I had to try them on, just once. When I put them on, I felt a slight nausea, but I decided it had nothing to do with the earrings and that it was simply my imagination. I continued wearing the earrings for some time after that. If only I had never put on those dreadful things! Perhaps they are the reason I'm here in this hospital now instead of at home. My point is that you have to be very careful with everything. The most innocent things could be the deadliest."

Erik thought back for a moment and remembered seeing his mother with a strange pair of emerald earrings. She had worn them when the entire family had gone to a party. He remembered her wearing a flashy golden dress and laughing with delight as she danced a waltz to the music of Strauss. Everyone had marveled at those earrings. Erik remembered admiring how beautiful his mother looked that evening. Now he wished that he could grind the two earrings into dust. And as he thought all these things, a new thought entered his mind. He remembered Taylor, the necklace, and the girl's dreams of the past . . .

Erik sat up straight in his chair. All traces of tears evaporated from his cheeks, and his eyes grew wide in shock. In that instant, he understood everything. Taylor had told him about three pieces of jewelry—a necklace, earrings, and a bracelet. They had seen the necklace at Mr. Chester's house. The location of the bracelet was still a mystery to him, but the earrings . . . the earrings were the very same pair of earrings his mother had worn to the party one year ago.

Chapter Fifteen

Taylor and the countess concluded their prayer and silence gathered around them. The countess wrapped her small, delicate fingers around the emerald stone and lifted it off the girl's forehead. The child stopped crying and a hush fell over her. Her breathing steadied and returned to a normal pace. With a soft sigh, the girl rolled over onto her side and fell asleep.

"This child's life is now out of danger," the countess said gently.

Taylor sighed happily, glad that she had been helpful. But a question formed in the girl's mind.

"Why," she asked quietly, "did you let me help you? You could have chosen any of your servants, but you chose me. Why me? I'm just an ordinary girl."

The countess shook her head and said, "To the eye, you are just an ordinary girl. But in my heart, I feel something strong residing within you. You have the power to do great things, my dear. All you have to do is believe in yourself."

She smiled at Taylor, who cast down her eyes. Her gaze fell upon the bracelet still on her wrist, and she gasped slightly. She fumbled with the bracelet until it slid off her wrist and lay in her palm. Taylor extended her hand toward the countess, returning the beautiful piece of jewelry. But the countess shook her head and, with her warm smile still in place, placed her hand on Taylor's and rolled the girl's fingers into a fist.

"Keep the bracelet. If you wish to help me cure victims of the disease, you must wear that bracelet. Just make sure you keep it safe."

"But," Taylor exclaimed, "this belongs to you! I don't deserve such a gift."

Still the countess refused to take back the bracelet. "Keep it, and hide it well. You shall need it yet . . ."

The entire day was hot and humid. Everyone stayed indoors, lounging in the dungeons of the castle where it was cool. Finally, the onset of evening brought a gentle breeze, and a chill quickly shrouded the land. Taylor gazed out from one of the immense windows and decided it would be wise to use this time while the cold winds blew to take a stroll through the castle gardens. To save time, she slid down the banister instead of taking the stairs and welcomed the cool rush of wind that greeted her face.

When she reached the foyer and burst through the door, she was shocked to discover she was the only person in the entire garden. It seemed strange that no one else had decided to take advantage of the evening chill. Taylor stretched and walked over to the stream that ran through the garden. Only the gurgle from the stream and the rustling of leaves broke the otherwise silent night.

Suddenly, Taylor heard the crunch of a footstep on the bank and whirled around to discover a dark silhouette heading straight toward her! Squinting, she recognized the figure as Erik, the count's son. She curtsied toward the dark figure, her eyes shining. "Your highness, I wish to thank you for all the help you've given me and the people of my village. Without your help, we would have surely starved," she said quietly.

"You are very welcome," the young man answered. "Besides, I got to meet you. That was certainly worth the trouble."

Erik smiled back at her with a kind gaze. His shoulder length brown hair waved gently in the breeze, and his clear brown eyes sparkled. Erik stepped closer to the girl and asked, "What is your name?"

"Taylor," she replied, her voice very soft.

"What a lovely name," Erik said. "Would you like me to show you around the castle? It would be a fine idea for you to get to know your way around. I have a feeling you may be staying here for a long time. It would be a great way for you to get to know your new home, don't you think?"

And what a fine way for me to get to know you, Taylor silently thought with a smile.

Chapter Sixteen

A door slammed downstairs. Taylor jerked out of her dream and rubbed the sleep out of her eyes. She had rested for only a very short time, but she wanted no more sleep. An abundance of cheery voices and happy laughter reached her ears, and she realized the rest of the family must already be up. Taylor dressed at top speed as her thoughts raced ahead to the day they were about to spend at Underground Atlanta. She allowed a quick smile to pass over her lips as she hurried downstairs to the kitchen where everyone was gathered.

"Taylor, please hurry up and eat your breakfast," Vicky shouted at her. "We've been waiting for you for hours! I've already walked the dog, prepared breakfast, and packed everything we will need for our trip."

Vicky's glare followed Taylor as she sat down at the kitchen table and started to wolf down her breakfast. "Be careful how long you sleep, dear," Vicky said. "If you let yourself, you could sleep forever!"

"No need to exaggerate," Sarah said. "We waited for Taylor for only half an hour."

Taylor grinned at her aunt's words. Sleep forever, indeed. She glanced up at Vicky, who was still scowling, and shook her head in disbelief at her aunt. Taylor knew her to be fifty, yet she looked as young as thirty-five. She was always strong in her words and actions and beautiful in her appearance. Even now, Taylor was amazed that her aunt had managed to prepare this entire meal in a matter of half an hour. The table was adorned with all kinds of wonderful foods including pancakes, sausage, fresh squeezed orange juice, and a huge fruit salad.

Suddenly, Taylor noticed Vicky's hands were clenched into fists. She eyed Taylor like a hawk stalking its prey, which convinced her that instead of examining her aunt, she should eat faster. Taylor smiled apologetically at her aunt and bent over her food once again.

Just as Taylor was about to eat her last bite of fruit, the telephone on the kitchen wall rang. Taylor reluctantly placed her fork back on her plate and picked up the telephone instead.

"May I speak to Taylor Creekmore, please?" a woman's voice asked cheerfully.

"This is Taylor. How may I help you?" Taylor replied.

"Taylor, my name is Cindy Ritten, and I'm calling from Kidzen Books. I know this is rather unusual and a last minute request, but I was wondering if you would be willing to do a book signing at our store today at noon. You see, we had scheduled a book signing with another author, but he can't make it because of bad weather conditions where he lives. He had planned to fly in this morning, but he can't get a flight out. Would you be willing to take his place?"

Taylor hesitated. "I don't know . . . our family was planning to spend the day at Underground Atlanta."

Cindy pleaded, "I know this is really last minute, but it would mean a lot if you would help us out. I can even send a car to pick you up." Hearing no answer, Cindy's plea became more desperate. "We really need someone to be here today. Please, if there is any way for you to come, I will be indebted to you. I promise you will be back home in two hours. Please, Taylor. I know the children would love you!"

Taylor heard an intake of breath on the other end of the line. She thought of the woman's worries and smiled at the possibility of helping her out of a jam.

"All right," she said at last. "I guess I could come, but I have to ask my parents first. Could you hold on a minute?"

Taylor turned away from the phone and called to her mother. "Mom, a lady is calling me about a book signing. She wants to know if I can be there at twelve o'clock today. The author who was scheduled can't get a flight into Atlanta. She says she will even send a car to come pick me up. Can I go?"

"Where is it, dear?" Sarah asked.

"At Kidzen Books. It's not far from here."

"Well . . ." Sarah began slowly.

"Don't worry, Mom. I'll be fine. You can still go to Underground Atlanta. I promise to come straight home afterward."

"All right, but make sure you take your cell phone in case you need to reach us," Sarah agreed.

Taylor ran up to Sarah and kissed her lightly on the cheek. Then, she ran back to the telephone and told the breathless Cindy she would be able to make it. She heard a loud sigh of relief from the other end of the line.

"Will you need me to send a car for you?"

"Yes, that would be perfect! And could I get a ride back home as well?"

Cindy was so relieved that Taylor was coming that she agreed to this last request without a single thought. "That would be no problem! Someone will be at your house by eleven to pick you up. Thank you for agreeing to do this on such short notice. May I speak with one of your parents now just in case they have questions?"

"Mom!" Taylor yelled. "The lady wants to talk to you!"

Sarah took the phone from her daughter and spoke briefly with Cindy. She handed the phone back to Taylor and said, "She just wanted to make sure it was okay with me. She also asked for our address so she could come pick you up."

Taylor could just imagine Cindy's big grin as she said, "Once again, thank you so much for agreeing to do this. I'll see you soon!"

"I'll see you at the store at noon," Taylor finished, and they both hung up.

As agreed, a Lexus sports utility vehicle roared up to the curb in front of Taylor's house five minutes to eleven. The silver door of the Lexus swung open and a pleasant, middle-aged woman stepped out. She pulled her black jacket tightly around her chest and adjusted the strap on one of her high-heeled red shoes. The woman walked quickly up the driveway with a worried look on her face. Upon seeing her, Taylor stepped outside to meet the woman.

"Are you Taylor?" the woman asked.

Taylor nodded her head and replied excitedly, "Yes, I am. Are you the person Cindy sent to pick me up for the book signing at Kidzen Books?"

The woman nodded her head and smiled. "Actually, I'm Cindy," she said. "I decided that instead of sending someone to pick you up, I would come myself."

She paused for a moment, deep in thought. After a few moments of silence, she voiced a question that seemed to be troubling her. "Have you ever done a book signing for kids before?"

"Yes, I have. In fact, I had one at Barnes and Nobles this past July. Don't worry. I know how to handle myself at a book signing, and I'm good with children."

"Well, that's perfect!" Cindy took Taylor by the arm and led her to the Lexus SUV. "Then you know all about reading parts of your novel to the kids. Are you comfortable answering their questions?"

"There is no need to worry. Really, I'll be fine. I know what to do," Taylor concluded and climbed into the back seat of the vehicle.

All the way from Taylor's house, Cindy questioned Taylor about her family, friends, school, and anything else that crossed her mind. Taylor also learned some things about Cindy. It turned out one of Taylor's language arts teachers had been Cindy's friend for a very long time. "Small world," Taylor commented.

"How are your math studies?" Cindy asked suddenly.

"So far, perfect! At least, I think so. So far I've received 100 percent on all of my math tests."

"In that case, maybe you can help me. My daughter, Rebecca, is also in ninth grade. She's having some difficulty with math. Do you think the two of you could get together sometime so you could help her with her math? Maybe she can help you with another subject in exchange. What do you say?"

"Oh, that would be no problem! I would love to help her. You can bring her over anytime."

"Thank you so much!" Cindy exclaimed. Taylor smiled when she saw the warm grin on the woman's face. Making someone happy always made Taylor feel good inside.

The miles quickly sped by and soon the Lexus stood outside a brick building. A yellow sign over the entrance read "Kidzen Books, The Children's Book Place." Over the sign was a picture of a boy with a book in his hands.

As soon as Taylor stepped inside, she saw a large poster of a man holding a book hanging from the ceiling. The caption beneath it read "George McKinney, author of *The Chronicles of Darksha*. See him here at Kidzen Books!" She assumed this was the author who was originally scheduled to appear today.

Cindy followed Taylor's glance and immediately apologized. "I'm sorry, Taylor. We simply didn't have enough time to change all the posters. But don't worry. It won't matter to the children. In fact, I think they'll like you even more than George McKinney. You're young, and they will relate a lot more to you than to an adult. And since you live in Alpharetta, that makes you a local celebrity. The children will be so excited to tell their friends all about this book signing and how they met you in person. Ah, children are starting to arrive now! Give

them a few minutes to get settled. Then introduce yourself, and the book signing will begin! Good luck!"

With that, Cindy headed toward the door to greet
her guests.

Chapter Seventeen

Taylor walked to the back of the store where a few kids were already assembled. She heard their excited whispers as they talked about the possibility of meeting her in person. Taylor tossed back her hair and stepped up on the small stage in front of which the kids were huddled. A wooden chair had been placed in the center of the stage for her.

"You can sit or stand," Cindy instructed when she joined Taylor again. "It doesn't matter as long as you are comfortable."

Taylor nodded at Cindy and sank down into the chair. She glanced up at the clock on the far side of the store and saw she still had twenty minutes until the start of the book signing. To pass the time, she allowed her eyes to roam around the room and smiled at every face she saw there. Taylor was amazed to see so many people there. Of course, the best part was that they were all there to see her.

But as Taylor sat there, she became a little worried. *What was I thinking? Of course they aren't here for me! All of the kids who came today came to see George McKinney, not Taylor Creekmore. What if they all leave when they discover another author has taken his place?*

Just then, Taylor heard a voice call out her name. "Taylor, Taylor Creekmore! Over here!"

Taylor stepped off the stage and looked around to see who it was. When she saw the person who had called her name, she gasped. It was Taylor's old friend, Kelly. The two girls looked at each other with delight, and it was difficult to say who was more overcome with joy. They had gone to school together before Taylor moved, and the two had been best friends. They had bid each other a sad farewell, but now with tears in their eyes, they ran to each other and hugged, crying with relief and laughing with joy at the same time.

When they calmed down, Kelly asked her old friend, "How've you been? It seems like forever since we last saw each other. I can't believe we just ran into each other like this! What are you doing here?"

Taylor laughed and hugged her friend again. "I've been doing fine, and I'm here because I have a book signing."

"Get out!"

"Really!"

"Wow! Oh, Taylor, I've missed you so much. It's too bad you had to move. I've made some new friends at school, but none of them could ever replace you."

"I know what you mean. I feel the same way."

"Well, if you feel the same way, then how come you haven't called me at all? I don't know your new phone number, and I haven't been able to contact you ever since you left."

"I'm so sorry! It's just that so many things have happened to me and I just . . . oh, I'm so sorry!"

"It's okay, but you have to promise to call me more often . . . way more often. Okay?"

"I promise."

"Great. Hey, listen, my parents just opened a new restaurant called Mozart." Suddenly, Kelly straightened up and took on a formal air. "Welcome to Mozart's palace of music, food, and entertainment." She dropped her professional tone and winked at her friend. "That just means welcome to our restaurant. I have to say it whenever someone walks in. I work as a waitress on Saturdays and Sundays. Why don't you and your family come this weekend? You can be my special guests."

"Cool! I know my parents would love to see your folks. I really love the name Mozart. He's one of my favorite composers. Does that mean that his music is played at the restaurant?"

"Uh huh! But I'm positive you'll like the food even more than the music."

"Is it really that good? I love Mozart's music so much that it'll be hard to beat!"

"Our food is amazing. You'll see!"

"Taylor!" Cindy called suddenly from behind the two girls. "It's time to get started."

"You go, girl!" exclaimed Kelly. "Hey, do you mind if I hang around and watch?"

Taylor shook her head. "Not at all. If you have an hour to spare, I could really use the support."

"Sure. You know you can count on me."

Taylor hugged her friend. "Thanks, Kelly."

When the two girls arrived at the back of the store, all of the children were already in place. They were all looking at the stage, eager for the book signing to begin. Taylor winked at them, and then motioned to Kelly to sit with the children. She walked onto the stage, sat down in the chair again, and took the copy of her book that Cindy handed her. Taylor smiled and greeted the children, "Hi! I'm Taylor Creekmore, and I wrote *The Galaxy Watch*. Have any of you heard of it?" Several hands went up in the air, including Kelly's.

Taylor continued, "That's great! So, would you like me to read some of it to you?"

"Yaah!"

With a smile, Taylor read the first chapter of her book. The children were attentive to her every word. When she finished, Taylor asked the children if they had any questions. Every hand shot up towards the ceiling, and Taylor felt a wave of warmth wash over her. Apparently, the children were just as interested in her as they were in McKinney. She acknowledged a little boy who sat in the front row. He pulled his black and red cap back and grinned up at her, his shiny eyes gleaming with excitement. His voice exploded as he asked the first question of the day.

"Why did you start to write books?"

A murmur filled the audience, and Taylor realized many of the kids had the same question. They all looked at her with wide-eyed anticipation.

"Well, when I was eleven and my sister was only five, I read day and night. My sister wanted to read the same books I read, but they were all too difficult for her. She would cry whenever I read the books because she wanted to read them too, but couldn't. So, I decided to write a story she could understand. Every day, I wrote a new story for her. When I finished the stories, my sister told me they would make a great book. I tied in the plots of each individual story, and they turned into a novel. That's how *The Galaxy Watch* was born."

The boy pushed his hat back on his head and stared thoughtfully at Taylor. She thought she saw something shine in his eyes and wondered if she had created a change in this boy, but that was soon forgotten as other kids asked questions.

After the question and answer period, Cindy told Taylor to move over to a table where the kids could bring their books for her to sign. As soon as Taylor picked up a pen, a little girl shoved a book under her nose. Taylor wrote a short note in the girl's book and then signed her name. The girl thanked the author and rushed off to find her mother.

Over the next half hour, the line of people waiting to get their books signed slowly dwindled. Finally, when Taylor's right hand cramped and ached from writing all those messages, only one more person was left. She looked up to see it was the boy in the red and black cap. He laid down his book before her and told her his name was Jonathan. Taylor personalized his copy and handed the book back to him. He took it in his hands but did not pull the book away. He held it for a while in silence, and then glanced up at Taylor. Their eyes met for an instant and the boy smiled. "One day," he said, "I'll be as great as you. You'll see."

"I'm sure you will. Good luck to you," Taylor said as she stood up.

Leaving the boy behind with the book, she found Kelly waiting for her at the front of the store. Putting the boy out of her mind, Taylor turned to Kelly. Her best friend's eyes sparkled with sheer joy.

"Oh, Taylor, I'm so happy for you! That was wonderful! I even bought a copy of your book. Are you going to write another one?"

"Actually, I'm already half done with my next book. This one's called *Moonpaw*. It should be in stores early next year."

"Oh, really? What's it about?"

"You'll find that out when you get the very first copy of my book!"

"Agreed."

They gave each other a final hug farewell before parting once more with a promise to meet again soon. But until that time, they would have to keep in contact more often. Of that Taylor was sure.

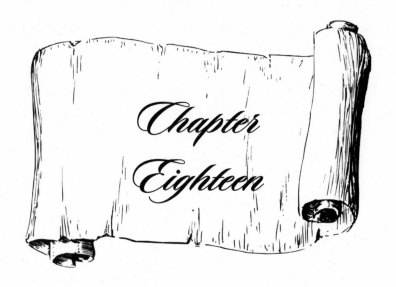

Chapter Eighteen

Cindy drove Taylor home as promised. The rest of the day passed swiftly and soon it was evening. Taylor sat with her family at the kitchen table, eating dinner and listening to her father's stories about the quality of his competitors' work.

" . . . and so he reached into the dishwasher, but poor Joey was just a beginner and forgot to disconnect the water hose. The dishwasher started spitting water like mad. So the floor is quickly flooding with water and the old lady is screaming like crazy. Then Joey tries to mop up the mess with some towels, but the old lady grabs a broom and starts walloping him on the back."

The whole family broke out laughing, and even Taylor allowed herself to join in the fun. Kyle took the opportunity to steal a piece of chocolate cake from his father's plate. Unfortunately, Amanda noticed and landed her fist right in the cake as she attempted to stop the theft. Both she and Kyle were splattered with chocolate, and everyone laughed again. Amanda giggled loudly and started trying to reach her nose with her tongue to lick off the chocolate, which only encouraged more laughter. Kyle shook his head to clear some cake from his hair before motioning to Taylor to come with him. Puzzled, she followed her cousin. Kyle went to the front door, scooping up Don's leash and securing it tightly to the dog's collar before opening the door and stepping outside. Taylor ran out after him.

The chilly night wind felt pleasant to Taylor. She spread out her arms and ran down to the street. As she ran, her hair billowed around behind her like a cloud, and she screamed with delight at the cool breeze. Kyle shook his head sadly and raced ahead to catch up with her.

"So, how did you like Underground Atlanta?" Taylor asked when Kyle finally caught up with her.

"It was amazing! I really loved it!"

"I like it, too. Atlanta really is a wonderful place to live. I remember when I lived in Los Angeles. There was trash all over the place. Newspapers littered the streets, and the houses were old and in disrepair. But Atlanta is neat and clean."

She paused for just a second, and her voice took on a somber tone as she asked, "How do you feel about moving here?"

"Well, my folks are buying that house, so I might as well like it. It's not like I could move back to Detroit by myself, is it?" Kyle said, his voice dripping with sarcasm.

Taylor glanced down sadly. That was just the thing her cousin was capable of. "You could always convince your parents to let you move back with one of your friends . . ."

The night air was suddenly filled with silence. Only the soft clicking of Don's sharp toenails against the hard asphalt could be heard.

Taylor suddenly felt the sharp pain of a pinecone hitting her shoulder. She rubbed her shoulder and looked over at Kyle, who was now standing under a pine tree. He laughed heartily and said, "Oh, come on, I wouldn't go back. If I did, who would take care of poor baby Taylor?"

But Kyle's happy smile was soon replaced with a look of despair. He turned slowly to his cousin and looked into her eyes. Taylor was shocked when she saw the depth of his seriousness. "Can I trust you with a secret?" Kyle asked.

"Of course," Taylor replied, eager to hear what had caused her cousin to change so.

Kyle sighed heavily and said, "I want to move back to Detroit. I know I can't, but I really, truly want to. You see, I have this girl back there. She's smart, talented, beautiful, and just . . ."

"Amazing?" Taylor suggested.

He nodded in reply. "Yeah, but now that we've moved, I'm afraid our relationship is ruined. I don't know when we will see each other again, and I'm afraid she's going to forget all about me. Sometimes, I can't help wondering if she has already begun to move on. When we first came down here, we talked every day for hours. Now, she never calls me, and every time I try to call her, she either can't come to the phone or she makes up some excuse to end the conversation quickly."

Kyle lowered his eyes to the ground and trudged on ahead, tossing the leash to Taylor. She felt so sorry for him. She knew how it felt to miss someone dear to you.

Glancing up at the sky, she imagined Erik's face for an instant, but then turned to her cousin who was clearly miserable and really needing someone to talk to. Suddenly, Taylor had an idea that just might help.

"It's time for you to start making some new friends down here. I ran into my best friend at the bookstore today. Her name is Kelly, and she's lots of fun. She invited us to visit the new restaurant her parents just opened. I think if you met her you would really like her."

"And how old is she?" Kyle asked, a slight hint of excitement in his voice.

"Right now, fifteen."

"Oh, she's young," he said sadly. After a pause, he asked, "What does she look like?"

"Well, she's really tall. She has all these dark curls that bob around her shoulders. Her hair goes well with her green eyes. She's really pretty."

"Wow! She sounds beautiful," Kyle whispered, and Taylor was delighted to hear the joy behind his words.

"And . . ."

"And what?" Kyle asked, confused.

"Is that all that interests you?" Taylor teased.

"What else is important?" he replied, scratching his head to hide his puzzlement.

"How about what she likes to do or what kind of personality she has?"

"I was just getting to that. So, go on, tell me everything! Maybe we can really become friends!"

Kyle and Taylor looked at each other and burst out laughing.

Chapter Nineteen

Erik couldn't believe it. If his mother's earrings and those of the countess were the same, it would certainly explain everything. Erik looked at his mother incredulously and asked, "You don't have a bracelet to go along with those earrings, do you?"

"A bracelet? Erik, what are you talking about?"

"Mother, please listen to me very carefully. This is very, very important." And with those words, Erik launched into his tale. He told her about his dreams of the future, Taylor's dreams of the past, the emerald necklace they saw on display, and of the terrible diseases the countess' jewelry gave to anyone who wears them. He saw the anguish in his mother's eyes, and he felt something stir deep within himself. A gentle voice spoke to him, telling him not to give up and to never lose hope! The gears of Erik's mind spun as he thought of a plan to change everything. If his plan worked, then his mother's life might be saved. Erik cracked a grin for the first time in many days. He was about to relay his plan to his parents, but then he stopped. They had enough to worry about already. There was only one person he could talk to about his mother's last hope . . .

$$\infty \quad \infty \quad \infty$$

Having just returned from school, Taylor sat at the wooden desk in her room, contemplating the next math problem on her worksheet. Vicky peered into the room and watched her scribble a few numbers down on the sheet. Finally, Vicky walked across the room and placed a hand on Taylor's paper. Taylor looked up, surprised at the interruption.

"Erik is downstairs. He wants to see you," Vicky explained. "He says it's urgent."

"Erik? Here?" Without waiting for an answer, Taylor threw her pencil on the desk and ran out of her room.

She saw Erik standing at the foot of the stairs. Her heart almost pounded out of her chest. How long had it been since she had last seen him? Oh, how she missed him! Just hearing his voice made her heart leap.

"Taylor . . . I . . . I'm so glad to see you," he said, smiling. Unfortunately, the smile did not seem to reach his eyes. Taylor flew across the landing toward him with her dark hair flying straight out behind her.

When Taylor came fully into view, Erik could not help notice what he had never seen in his friend before. There was hidden beauty in her, as well as great power. And that smile . . . he would do anything for that smile. By the glow in her eyes, he could tell that she liked him, too. She was perfect. There was no other word for her. Perfect . . .

"Erik! I'm so happy you're back. Why didn't you let me know you were coming? When did you get back? You didn't even warn me . . . is something going on? And don't try to play dumb. A guy doesn't return from the other side of the country just to pay a visit to a friend."

The two teenagers walked into the living room and sat down on the sofa. Erik placed his head in his hands, avoiding Taylor's gaze. For a moment, Taylor was not sure what to do. Just as she reached to console Erik, he raised his head and, in a flash of understanding, Taylor realized something was troubling him.

"Erik, what's the matter? Something's wrong, and I know it. Please, please tell me. I promise I'll do anything I can to help. But I can't help you if I don't know what's going on."

"Taylor, it's my mother. She's dying of cancer. She's been doing chemotherapy, but it's not working. The doctors haven't given her much time to live. They can't give us an exact time. All they know is time's running out."

Taylor could feel her heart breaking as she heard the desperation in Erik's voice. *Time is running out . . .* such terrible words! Tears filled her eyes and began to trickle down her cheeks. She opened her mouth to say something, but only a small sob came out.

Erik looked heartbroken, but he steeled himself for the next words. Very slowly, he whispered, "But . . . but that's not the whole story. Taylor, my mom has the countess' earrings."

Taylor's tears froze on her face. *The countess' earrings? Impossible! It's crazy! And yet . . . and yet . . . it could be true. Although it's a crazy thought, it could be true.* Finally, she said, "Are you sure they are the countess' earrings? Did your mother wear them?"

"She wore them once to a party about a year ago. After that, she began to feel ill and dizzy. I'm afraid they caused her cancer. But I have an idea. Taylor, I believe we could save my mother's life if we could . . ."

"If we could find the bracelet . . . "

" . . . and steal the necklace . . ."

"Then we could save your mother! Oh, Erik!" Taylor exclaimed. Suddenly, her voice lowered sadly. "Of course, that's a pretty big if. I mean, how will we ever find the bracelet? What if we can't find it? What will we do then?"

But Erik had no time for doubts. He grabbed Taylor's hands and pressed them together. "We can try. We can always try. And if we don't make it . . . well, then at least we'll know we tried. That's better than giving up. But I'll need your help. I can't do this alone."

No words seemed fit to reply. Taylor could see the fiery determination in Erik's eyes. She felt his fingers burn with hope. She broke free of all her restraints and wrapped her arms around him. Her courage and strength flowed from her body into his as she whispered, "I would never, ever let you do something like this alone. I'll be there every step of the way."

Suddenly, a gentle voice came from the entrance to the living room. "Is everything okay?" Vicky asked. "I thought I heard someone crying. What's wrong?"

Taylor wiped tears from her eyes and turned towards her aunt. "Erik's mother is dying of cancer."

"Oh, no! Erik, I'm so sorry."

Erik relayed the whole story to Vicky. Tears swelled in her eyes, and she began to cry when she learned that nothing could be done. But through her tears, she managed to stammer a few words of encouragement. "I'm sure your mother will be all right. I don't know how, but I know it will happen. I feel it in my heart."

Taylor and Erik exchanged a frightened glance.

Chapter Twenty

Erik led Taylor to one of the vast stone walls of the castle. He ran his hand along the wall, and he smiled gently. "This is the oldest part of the castle. And these," he motioned to the two towers standing on either end of the wall, "you shall find out about very soon."

The two towers were of equal width and height. Each loomed far above the top of the wall and cast vast shadows over the ground. Erik led Taylor to the left tower. She kept staring upward, trying to see the top of the tower. The tallest building in her small village was only two stories high.

Taylor hardly noticed the door in the tower until she bumped up against it. Rubbing her shoulder, she reached for a doorknob or a handle, but her fingers simply touched wood. When she took a closer look, Taylor was amazed to discover there was no doorknob at all. *Why build a door that can't be opened?* she wondered.

But Erik walked around her and pointed to a small window carved in the wooden door. There were six metal bars set into the edges of the window. Three of the bars ran horizontally and three ran vertically. Erik grabbed the middle horizontal bar and pulled it outward. He then turned it ninety degrees, first to the left and then to the right. Finally, he pushed the bar back in place. The door swung open silently on well-oiled hinges.

Erik entered the dreary room and removed a lit torch from its bracket on the wall. The blaze illuminated the dark chamber, revealing a set of stone steps that curved upward and out of sight. Taylor supposed they led to the top of the tower. Indeed, when they ascended and emerged through a trapdoor, they were surrounded by a view the likes of which she had never imagined. To one side of the castle was the sea, roaring, churning, and always shifting. To the other side was a still, motionless forest. She placed her hands on the rough edges of the tower and glanced over the edge at the infinite darkness below.

She heard Erik's voice behind her telling her about the tower. " . . . and that's where the watchmen would stand. They would constantly be on the lookout for enemies or any sign of danger. Of course, that was in the past. There is no need for watchmen now."

Taylor looked up and turned her head to get a better view. She stretched out her hand. The forests surrounding the castle could have been right in her palm. They were that close. She actually stretched out her fingers and tore a leaf off an oak that grew near the wall. Taylor threw the leaf into the wind and watched as a breeze carried it away. For a minute, she forgot her weariness and savored the moment, wishing it would last forever. The distant howling of a wolf and the hoot of an owl sounded like friends. She was one with the world, all worries forgotten. She was one with the wild.

Far overhead, the clouds shifted away from the moon, which cast a glow upon the castle grounds.

"Did you hear that?" Erik asked suddenly. His voice sounded vague and distant in Taylor's dream world.

"Only the howling of a lone wolf."

"No, not that. I'm sure I heard someone yell."

Taylor tore her thoughts back to the present to see a man sprinting across the courtyard. Erik shouted something at the man and ran down the steps leading from the tower after him. Taylor dashed after Erik.

It all happened in an instant. The smooth steps transformed into a death trap as Taylor's foot caught on a crack in the stone. Suddenly, she was falling toward what seemed to be certain doom. A scream passed her lips, and she saw a whirl of color before her eyes. Then it was over. She was safe in a pair of strong hands that held her tightly and pulled her back to her feet. Erik smiled at her and motioned to the doorway below. They ran down the remaining steps together.

Erik flung open the door and cast his eyes around the courtyard. It was empty. Erik shook a fist and muttered a few indiscernible words before turning about face and running back to the castle's main gate. Taylor quickly followed suit, eager to discover who the strange man was and why he was fleeing the castle in such a hurry.

It did not take long for Erik and Taylor to discover the man's identity. When they ran into the main hall, they saw the countess was there as well. Her husband stood beside her, cursing the man. He paused for a moment to question the soldiers who were just now entering the chamber.

"Who saw him? Does anyone know who this man is? Someone must have gotten a good look at him!"

"Chester . . ." the countess whispered softly.

"Chester?" he yelled back.

"Yes, Chester. He stole my necklace. I . . . I recognized him when he tore the necklace from my neck. Then, he raced off to who knows where." Her voice quavered, but her eyes blazed with both fire and ice. The sight of the countess' anger frightened Taylor.

"But he shall not get away with this!" the countess continued. "Never shall he forget this night, nor shall he ever cease to regret this terrible deed. He took the necklace and is happy now, but from this day forth, he shall never know peace again. This day, he has cut his own life short by taking what was not his. Let a curse rage upon Chester!" she cried, arms stretched toward the sky and eyes filled with fiery sparks. "Let the necklace be cursed! For all eternity, let it be cursed!"

So strong was the countess' anger that Taylor felt a wave of dark passion sweep over her. The girl withdrew from the menacing woman, feeling small and unimportant in the presence of the countess' power. But then a tiny voice spoke in the back of Taylor's mind. *The bracelet,* it whispered. She glanced down and saw the shimmering emeralds sparkling on her wrist and decided that now was the time to return it to the countess. Her need for it was now greater than Taylor's. Summoning up all her courage, Taylor stepped forward and extended the bracelet toward the countess.

Taylor felt the wave of anger recede as the woman's eyes fell upon the bracelet. Although she could still feel the air burning with the countess' hatred, the fire in her eyes was gone. Her gaze softened, and she smiled at the girl standing before her. She took the bracelet from Taylor's hand and slipped it back on the girl's wrist.

"No, you keep it. May it forever bring you joy, happiness, and peace. Keep it as a memory. Keep it as a gift. May this bracelet forever bless you."

"But . . ."

The countess shook her head, silencing Taylor. "There is something you must remember," she said. "If you ever find the necklace, you must keep it with you at all times. Don't forget that . . . always keep it with you. Make sure it never falls into the wrong hands. But don't wear it, else the curse will descend upon you."

"But . . ."

"Hush, child. Go now, and allow me to deal with the rest. Just remember what I said, and may luck shine on your life forevermore."

Chapter Twenty-One

Taylor wrapped the telephone cord around her index finger and pressed the black phone against her ear. She heard ringing at the other end of the line as she pulled down the blind on the window next to where she was sitting. The sun was getting in her eyes, and she had no time for interruptions. She drummed her fingers against the kitchen countertop and waited for Kelly to pick up.

"Hello?" came Kelly's voice at last. Taylor could just imagine the confused expression of her friend's face when she saw an unknown number on her cell phone.

"It's me, Taylor."

Taylor heard a sharp intake of breath from the other end of the line. "Taylor? Oh, wow! It's good to hear from you! What's up?"

"What's up with you?"

Kelly gave a big sigh. "I have so much homework today. I wish you still lived near me. Then, at least we could hang out together while we do our homework. I'd even let you do some of mine," Kelly giggled.

Typical Kelly, Taylor thought, shaking her head. "Well, how about taking a break from all that work. Want to hear something funny that happened at school today?"

Kelly's tone of voice changed from dull to excited in an instant. "Oh, yeah! You know how much I love your stories. I hope this one's really funny!"

"I think you'll like it. It's about the boy who guessed."

"The boy who guessed?" Kelly asked in confusion.

"We had an exam in history today. Everyone was working as usual. The test was kinda hard and everyone was really concentrating, but this one kid, Ryan, went up to the teacher just five minutes after she handed out the test and turned in his paper. When the teacher looked it over, she saw he had circled the letter A on all the multiple-choice questions. When she asked him why, he told her he had just guessed. So, she told him to take his test back to his desk and do it again. When he brought his test up again, all he had done was erased all of the As and circled B for all the questions. This really made the teacher mad. She told Ryan if he didn't go back and answer each question properly, she would send him to the principal's office. So guess what he did that time."

"Guessed?" Kelly suggested.

"You've got it! But this time, he alternated his answers between C and D."

Kelly laughed. "Did she send him to the principal's office?"

"Oh, yeah! He got suspended for three days. Can you believe it? But I think from this day forward, Ryan will always be known as the boy who guessed!"

Another giggle came from the other end of the line. "You know, that reminds me of a funny story of my own. In fact, I'm on punishment because of it."

"Punishment? For what?"

"Well, since you left, I started this habit of coming home and locking myself in my bedroom. It's not like I'm not doing anything bad or dangerous. I'm just listening to music, talking on my cell phone, or instant messaging my friends. But my parents got really tired of it, so they warned me to stop locking my bedroom door. I guess they're worried that I might be doing drugs or something, which is crazy because they should know I'm not like that. Anyway, I ignored them. I wasn't doing anything wrong, you know. Like what's the big deal, anyway? I figured they couldn't do anything to stop me. Boy, was I wrong! Would you believe they unhinged my door?"

"No!"

"Yes! They literally took my door off the hinges to stop me from locking myself in. And the worst part is my dad hid the door somewhere. I can't find it anywhere! I looked all over the house—the attic, the basement, and the garage—nothing. If this goes on, I'll have to wander the streets with a sign that says 'Got Door?'"

Taylor could not contain herself. She laughed so hard tears began to well up in her eyes. Just thinking about Kelly walking door to door with a 'Got Door?' sign around her neck was too funny.

Right then, Taylor heard Amanda calling her by tapping two plastic toys together. It was their traditional way to begin playtime. Taylor sighed apologetically. "I'm really sorry, but I've got to go now. Thanks for making me laugh. Good luck on your homework!"

"Luck won't have anything to do with it," Kelly finished mysteriously and hung up. Taken aback by this sudden change in her friend, Taylor sighed again and placed the telephone back on its stand. *Maybe some things are better left unknown,* Taylor thought as she made her way to Amanda.

Later that evening, Taylor was so tired when she finally went to bed that her head scarcely touched the pillow before she fell asleep.

Chapter Twenty-Two

"Taylor!" Erik whispered excitedly. "Taylor, wake up! Hurry! Something important has happened! Get up!"

Taylor tossed off her blanket and rubbed her eyes sleepily. It was still early in the morning, and the castle was very quiet. Motioning for her to be absolutely silent and to follow him, Erik crept out the open door. Taylor followed, not caring that she was still in her nightgown.

Erik led the way through several dark and silent hallways before the sounds of frightened voices reached their ears. Puzzled, Taylor moved faster. After a few more minutes of walking, they reached the source of the voices.

The count and the countess, along with a number of other people, were gathered around a fallen statue of a woman and a vase in the hallway that led from the dining chamber. The people around her were talking in scared voices about spirits and curses. At first, Taylor didn't understand what the fuss was about, but when a couple in front of her moved aside, she gasped in terror.

Lying inches from the fallen vase was a young man.

"Who is he?" Taylor asked Erik.

"It's Chester," he said solemnly, "the man who stole my mother's necklace."

Taylor nodded sadly and glanced back at the young man. But this time, her eyes landed on his head and she turned away in horror. She recognized him as the figure she had seen in the courtyard, but that was not what made her turn away in terror and sadness, nor was it what made her cry out in tears. The young man's head was pierced, and a single trickle of dark blood flowed steadily down the side of his head.

Days turned into weeks and weeks into months as time flew by. The toll of time was most reflected in Erik's mother, whose health was steadily declining. Erik was not only worried about the steady loss of time, but he was also consumed with getting the necklace. He knew where to find it, but had no idea how to get it away from Mr. Chester. He had considered simply asking the old man, but feared Mr. Chester would not be willing to part with his valuable treasure so easily. Many explanations would be needed, and Mr. Chester would certainly not believe the truth. So Erik had to come up a plan that would allow him to safely secure the necklace without letting Mr. Chester know what he was up to.

After weeks of pondering the problem, Erik believed he had finally come up with a solution, but he couldn't do it alone. He would need help, and he knew just the person to call. Erik walked to the phone and quickly dialed a familiar number. His heart thumped as he listened to the ringing at the other end of the line. Erik shook his fist in anger when an answering machine picked up.

"Hello, and thank you for calling. You have reached the . . ." The message was interrupted when someone picked up the phone. "Dumb machine," Erik heard the person say. "Always picks up before I can get to the phone. Anyway, thank you for calling. Can I help you?"

"Grandpa?" Erik asked and laughed.

"Who's this?"

"It's Erik. I was just calling to see how you were feeling."

With a bit of a chuckle in the old man's voice, he said, "Why, I've been feeling fine. I'm great, actually."

"So what do you think about this weather we've been having? I think it's great!"

Erik heard laughter, and his grandfather said, "How about you just skip to the point, lad. If you are calling me, then it must be for something more important than my health or the weather."

Erik's grandfather had worked his whole life as a professional jeweler. He was a master craftsman who created copies of famous pieces of jewelry. His services were used mostly by museums when they wanted to send a copy of a precious artifact to other museums around the world. Erik's grandfather's work was so excellent that it was nearly impossible to decipher the difference between his copy and the real thing. As he poised himself to ask for his grandfather's help, he couldn't help but feel stupid for not thinking of it sooner.

"All right, you got me. Grandpa, I need your help. My friend Taylor and I recently visited a private exhibit of some ancient jewelry."

"Really? How interesting," his grandfather said. After a moment, he added, "Say now . . . you wouldn't be talking about old Chester's exhibit, now would you?"

"That's the one!"

"Oh, I saw that exhibit too. What stunning pieces! My favorite was that beautiful emerald necklace at the very end. Wasn't it amazing?"

"Oh, yes, it was quite special. In fact, that's the reason for my call. Taylor really loved that necklace. I was just wondering if you could make a copy that I could give her for her birthday. I would really like to surprise her with it. I know it will just blow her away. Would you make a copy for me?"

"Now is that something to ask of your old grandpa?" Erik drew in a breath, afraid he may have upset his grandfather. His worry was in vain, however. His grandfather laughed again and said, "Oh, I'm just fooling with you. I would be delighted to craft a necklace for your friend. When is her birthday?"

"In a month, but the sooner I can get it the better."

"Not to worry. I can have it ready in a week, if you can get me a picture of it."

"I have a picture from the newspaper. I can bring it over today."

"Great! Just don't forget about it."

"Thanks, Grandpa!"

"Anything for my favorite grandson."

The rest of the week was spent in turmoil. Erik paced around the house, eager for the days to fly by. Even school and spending time with Taylor could not distract him from his fears. *What if something went wrong?* Erik was trusting his mother's fate to pure luck. He didn't like it at all, but he had no other choice. No amount of thoughtful consideration would change that fact. Fate would have to be his guide this time.

Finally, the long awaited phone call came. Erik's grandfather had finished the necklace at last.

Erik grabbed his keys and rushed out of the house. He snatched open the car door and jumped in. Jamming his keys into the ignition, he roared out of the driveway and raced down the street. He was sweating now. In a short while, he would be at his grandfather's and pick up the necklace. He turned the corner, thundered onto the main road, sped up the car and screeched to a halt in the midst of a dead traffic jam.

"Great," Erik moaned.

Several long, painstaking hours later, Erik's car finally came to a stop in front of his grandfather's house. Without even stopping to apply the parking brake, Erik pulled the keys from the ignition and dashed to the door, jumping over his grandfather's beloved daisies along the way. The old man opened the door as soon as Erik's fist made the first knock.

"Grandpa!"

Erik's grandfather hugged him warmly and welcomed the young man inside.

"So, where is it?" Erik asked quickly.

"Calm down, boy, before you have a heart attack from all that excitement! I've got it in the living room," he replied before going off into another room.

The old man returned in a minute, carrying the sparkling necklace with him. *It's almost better than the original,* Erik thought as his grandfather handed him the necklace.

"Wow, I can't believe it! It's perfect! They sure don't call you a master jeweler for nothing, Grandpa. You don't know how much this means to me!"

But as Erik wrapped his arms around his grandfather, in the back of his mind he had only one thought. *You really don't know what this means . . .*

Chapter Twenty-Four

Soon after the family from Detroit made their offer on the house, the offer was accepted. Several weeks after that Vicky, Michael, and Kyle finally accomplished their goal. They officially moved to Georgia! Now, Vicky sat in Alex's office as his secretary, Alex and Michael fixed appliances, and Kyle worked as an apprentice to learn the trade.

Sarah and Taylor assisted Vicky with unpacking the family's possessions when they arrived from Detroit. All week, they had taken various things out of their boxes and placed them throughout the house. Now, they stood in the entry hall, arguing over the perfect spot to hang an old, worn tapestry. Sarah didn't want to hang it at all, but Vicky argued it was a family relic and deserved to be hung in a special spot. The tapestry was so old that it was almost impossible to discern the original colors, but the people's faces still peered down as if they were scoffing at humanity. In the end, it was decided the best place for the tapestry would be above the living room fireplace where everyone who entered the house could admire it.

Unfortunately, as soon as this problem was resolved, Vicky managed to unearth another to take its place. Taylor sighed as Vicky unwrapped a rag from a statue. She loved looking at all the antiques her aunt possessed, but when it came to placing them around the house, she would rather be anywhere but here. Vicky always took forever to choose a place for each treasure. It seemed that every piece had been passed down from generation to generation in her family and thus each had to be in the perfect place for everyone to see it.

Eventually, every item found its rightful place. And although Vicky was still unhappy about some of the placements, Taylor was just glad the job was finally complete. She flopped down on the leather sofa and stretched out her tired arms and legs.

"It's too bad the men weren't here to help us," Vicky sighed sadly and wiped a bit of dust off her shirt.

"Well, I think Michael and Kyle will get a very pleasant surprise when they get home," Sarah commented. "The books are on the shelves, the paintings on the walls, and the tapestry is in the living room above the mantelpiece. In my opinion, it's absolutely beautiful!"

Beautiful, yes, Taylor thought sleepily. *Enjoyable work, no . . .*

Chapter Twenty-Five

Mr. Chester's rocking chair creaked as the old man sat down heavily. From the back porch, he cast his eyes over the place where the old oak had once stood and sighed heavily. He missed his old friend.

Suddenly, Mr. Chester heard the phone in the kitchen clatter on its stand. He pulled himself up from the chair and hobbled over to the kitchen table where the phone rested. Lifting the handset to his ear, he announced, "This is Robert Chester. How may I help you?" *I hope this isn't another one of those telemarketers,* he thought, shaking his head.

A man's voice issued from the phone. "Hello, Mr. Chester. I'm calling because I believe I may have unearthed something you might like." The voice paused, and Mr. Chester took the moment to nervously run his fingers through his hair. A second later, the man continued. "I have recently discovered a pair of earrings that match the emerald necklace you have on display."

"A pair of earrings, did you say?"

"Yes. Perhaps we could schedule a time for me to come by and show you the earrings."

Ambitious young man, aren't you, thought Mr. Chester. "Well, the exhibit is closed right now . . ."

"That's not a problem. I'm not interested in seeing the exhibit. I just wanted to allow you an opportunity to examine the earrings for yourself. You will know if they match the necklace. I am sure you will be quite surprised."

Chester raised his eyebrows in suspicion. *Why does he want to get into my house?* Chester thought. Carefully, he asked, "Who are you?"

"That doesn't really matter, sir. If you will just allow me to show you . . ."

"What kind of fool do you take me for? Do you have any proof of what you are saying?"

"I . . . yes . . ."

"And what would that be?"

"Let me come by, and I'll show you."

Mr. Chester heard the urgency in the man's voice. *There is certainly something odd about this . . .*

"Let me show you," the man repeated.

I suppose it won't hurt to see the earrings, thought Mr. Chester. "All right, you may come by. I can see you in half an hour. Can you be here by then?"

"Sure. Not a problem. I'll see you then. Thank you! You won't be sorry!"

Half an hour later, Erik was standing before Mr. Chester's wooden door. He rang the doorbell and backed up, balancing on the balls of his feet. One wrong move and his entire plan would fail. But at least part one had been a success. He had gotten himself invited into Mr. Chester's house. Now for part two.

The same beautiful lady who had welcomed him last time opened the door. He nodded to her as he walked in and quickly shifted his thoughts to the work at hand. Erik hardly heard the girl as she said, "Welcome, young man. Have a seat, and I shall inform Mr. Chester that you are here. In the meantime, can I get you something to drink? Tea, or perhaps a cup of coffee?"

"No, but thank you for the offer," Erik replied. She nodded and silently withdrew to another room.

In a few minutes, Mr. Chester entered the room. He smiled at Erik and extended his hand. "Good day to you. I assume you are the gentleman who called about the earrings. Is that correct?"

Erik accepted the old gentleman's hand and nodded. He then reached into one of his pockets and gingerly lifted out a small velvet box. Inside the box, lying on a sheet of red velvet, lay a pair of silver earrings with beautiful emerald stones. Mr. Chester snatched the box from the young man's grasp and lifted it to eye level. From his pocket, he drew a shiny gold monocle and pressed it up to his eye. He examined the earrings for a very long time. Erik was sure his heart would leap out of his chest. After several long and tense minutes, Chester handed the box back to Erik. Apparently, the earrings passed the old man's test.

"Yes, these are a perfect match to my necklace. I have no doubt the same master crafted both of these pieces."

"Oh, really? I have to tell you I was even a bit skeptical about it myself at first," Erik whispered. He was faking his surprise, but it was all part of the plan. "That's why I came to see you. I wanted to know for sure."

"Would you like to see the necklace? I assure you, they are of one set, but if you wish, I can show it to you."

"If it wouldn't be too much of a bother . . ."

Mr. Chester smiled and said, "Very well, follow me."

The old man led Erik down a long corridor. Erik realized this was not the same path he had taken on his first visit to the house. As they walked, Chester turned to Erik and asked, "By the way, where did you get those earrings?"

Erik was buried so deeply in his thoughts that he hardly heard the old man. At length, he replied, "They're my mother's."

"Oh . . ." Mr. Chester replied slowly, and Erik was horrified to hear the distrust in the man's voice.

They emerged in a small office. The room was furnished with a tiny table, a chair, a bookcase built into the wall, and a dusty old rug on the floor.

"Sit down, young man," Mr. Chester instructed, motioning toward the chair. Erik lowered himself gently into the seat, afraid of breaking the fragile antique.

Erik felt his heart hammering painfully. He was certain the old man would hear his heart thundering, realize what he was really up to, and throw him out of the house. Then, his only chance of saving his mother would be gone. He forced himself to calm down. He would not allow his plan to be disrupted.

Then another thought hit Erik. *What if Mr. Chester changed his mind about showing him the necklace?* He swallowed and looked at Mr. Chester breathlessly.

Luckily, the man paid no attention to Erik and instead focused on the bookshelf. Mr. Chester grabbed one of the books and pulled it out. The bookshelf slid forward, and Erik was surprised to see a small passageway behind the shelf. It was just wide enough for one man to fit inside. Chester glanced back at Erik to be sure the youth did not follow and slipped behind the bookshelf. The young man heard the clicking of a lock and the gentle clicking of a safe opening. It wasn't long before Mr. Chester returned to the room with the necklace in hand. He placed a velvet pad on the table and laid the necklace on it.

"Now you may compare your earrings with the necklace. Take a good look, young man. Are you convinced now?"

Erik placed the shining emerald earrings next to the necklace. The moment the earrings touched the velvet, a spark seemed to shoot between the two pieces of jewelry. A blaze sparkled for a single instant in the necklace's emerald, but then it faded and all was still. He faked a gasp of surprise and pressed his hand over his mouth. "You're right. They are of the same set. Well, that is an unexpected surprise."

Mr. Chester furrowed his eyebrows. "Unexpected? But on the phone you said you believed them to be of one set! What is this? What's going on here?"

Erik racked his brains for a response. It was true what they said. The problem with lying is you have to remember what you said to whom. You don't have to worry about messing up the truth because it's always the same. Erik decided to take the innocent approach. Clearing his throat and looking up with wide eyes, he replied, "Well, like I told you before, what I said on the telephone was only a hunch. I didn't really believe what I was saying. It's only now that I'm truly convinced the earrings and the necklace really are from one set."

As Erik spoke, he was already thinking of how to fulfill the third and final step of his plan. He needed to somehow distract the old man from his precious piece of jewelry. But because Chester stayed so close to the necklace, it was unlikely his eyes would stray from it until it was back in the safe. It seemed his plan was destined to fail after all.

Luckily, it was at that moment that the beautiful young woman who worked for Mr. Chester knocked on the office door. She stuck her head inside and smiled at the elderly man.

"Excuse me, Mr. Chester. There's someone here to see you. Apparently, it's quite urgent."

Mr. Chester apologized to Erik and promised to be back in a few minutes. Erik nodded and smiled back at Mr. Chester as he walked out the door. The moment Mr. Chester had fully vanished, Erik's smile was replaced with a look of grim determination. He pulled out the necklace his grandfather had made for him and held it up to the real one for a final examination. They were identical. Perfect!

Erik carefully lifted the genuine emerald necklace from the velvet and slowly put his makeshift version in its place. Making sure the necklace on the velvet pad was in the exact same position as when Mr. Chester left the room, Erik slipped the real one into his pocket. Now all he could do was sit, wait, and hope that the old man did not detect any difference. He knew that if Mr. Chester discovered the necklace on the pad was a forgery, the old man would have him arrested immediately.

Luck served Erik again when the old man returned. Without even looking at Erik, he lifted the necklace to eye level and smiled at the shine of the stone and the sparkle of the beautiful chain. Handing the earrings back to Erik, Mr. Chester thanked him for coming. But before he let the young man leave, he asked, "By the way, I'm very interested in adding those earrings to my collection. Are they for sale?"

"I'm sorry, but no. If I ever decided to sell them, I promise to contact you first."

Mr. Chester nodded and quickly bid him farewell without a second thought. Erik did not breathe freely, however, until he was in his car with the door locked.

Chapter Twenty-Six

The day of Taylor's birthday was approaching swiftly. The sky was spotless with not even a hint of a cloud. The breeze was cool and brisk and the sun warm and bright. Ironically, everyone and everything about this day was joyous except the birthday girl herself.

Taylor had no desire to celebrate anything, least of all her own birthday. She did not want to be with anyone, except perhaps Erik. Sarah was happy that Taylor was at least still amicable with Amanda, Kyle, Erik, and her best friend, Kelly. Sarah decided to have just a small party with their family, Vicky, Michael, Kyle, Kelly, and Erik's family.

Fortunately, a phone call from Kelly helped relieve Taylor's foul mood.

"Hey Taylor! How are you?"

"I'm all right."

Concern resounded in Kelly's voice. "Are you sure? You don't sound all right. What's wrong?"

For one moment, Taylor was ready to pour out everything to Kelly. She wished her friend would cry with her, mourn with her, and reassure her that all would turn out all right. But the moment passed, and she decided to allow Kelly to remain ignorant of her affairs for a little longer. So instead of a long, drawn out reply about Erik's mother, the emerald jewelry, her dreams, the spirits, and the countess, Taylor simply said, "Nothing's wrong. I'm fine. What's going on with you?"

Kelly was not at all convinced that her friend was fine, but she decided to let it slide. It was clear that Taylor was not ready to confide in her. So instead, she said, "Everything is good with me . . . well, almost everything."

Taylor was relieved that Kelly didn't push. Kelly knew her well enough to know she was hiding something, and she appreciated her friend's patience. Now, it was Taylor's turn to be concerned about what was happening in Kelly's life.

"What do you mean by almost everything?"

"Lets just say I had a few issues with a fire drill."

"A fire drill? How can you have issues with a fire drill?"

Kelly sighed sadly. "Well, it wasn't really a fire drill. It was actually a fire *alarm*."

Taylor couldn't suppress a gasp of disbelief. "You mean there was a real fire? Where? When?"

"At school today. It all started in my political science class. We were watching a video about the judicial system. We were right at the part where a policeman was demonstrating the capture of a drunk driver. The teacher had also given us this worksheet to go along with the movie, so most of us had our heads down."

"Okay, but what does that have to do with a fire alarm?"

"If you would give me a second, I'll get to it. At that moment, we heard a shrill sound like a whistle and a white light started flashing in the classroom. We thought it was the policeman in the video attempting to stop the driver, so we went on with our work. Even the teacher ignored the alarm. She was busy working on her computer."

Taylor could not help but comment, "Oh, I think I see where this is going . . ."

"After a minute or so of this flashing light and the siren blasting, I began to suspect something was wrong. I finally looked up from my worksheet and glanced at the television screen and saw the driver sitting behind bars in jail. The policeman was grinning, holding the guy's driver's license. The chase scene had long ended, but the siren and lights persisted. That's when I realized it was a fire drill. I did the only thing I could. I ran up to the front of the class, stood with my arms out in front of the television screen, and yelled, 'Fire drill! Fire drill! Everybody out!'

"You can imagine the joy my classmates felt at having to leave the classroom for what they considered was a waste of time. Two kids in the back of the room actually threw spitballs at me. Everyone was complaining until the teacher looked up from her computer and said, 'There's no fire drill scheduled for today.' That's when everyone panicked. Chairs and papers went flying as everyone rushed for the door. It finally hit everyone that this was no drill. It was the real thing. People ran screaming down the halls. All you could see was a mass of bodies scrambling frantically toward the nearest exit. It was crazy because despite all those fire drills we have, no one was prepared for a real fire. All thoughts of exiting in an orderly manner were forgotten. The only thing that mattered was escaping from a burning school."

Taylor felt fear and pity welling up in her throat. She couldn't imagine how frightened those poor people had to be. As she listened, she started hoping this story would have a happy ending. Taylor pressed Kelly by asking, "What happened?"

Hearing the worry and anxiety in Taylor's voice, Kelly gave a short laugh. "Oh, don't worry," she said. "It turned out all right. The students were all huddled outside the school, looking for smoke and listening for fire trucks. But none of us could have ever guessed what caused the fire."

"How did it start?"

"It was all the fault of this one student named Mark Chester. He is one of the worst students in the entire school. Mark steals, tears up school property, and is always starting fights. All the students and teachers hate him. He's constantly in detention and has even been suspended a few times."

Taylor shifted in her chair anxiously. *Why would anyone start a fire?* She was all ears when Kelly continued.

"Mark had a math final today. He's always been a terrible student, but he usually tried a little bit on his exams. But for some reason, he decided he just didn't feel like trying today. He just drew all over the page until Mrs. Krick, the math teacher, announced the end of the test and told all the students to bring their tests to her desk. Mark threw his paper on her desk and slumped back down in his seat.

"When Mrs. Krick saw Mark's paper, she decided she had had enough. She held Mark's paper above her head and shouted, 'Mark Chester, I've had enough from you. You will redo this test right now or I'll have you expelled!'

"The entire class looked at Mark in disbelief. He just sat there, twiddling his thumbs and staring up at the ceiling. Then, his lips started moving, but no one heard what he said. Mrs. Krick repeated her warning, but Mark didn't move. Finally, he said, 'Change my answers for me, Mrs. Krick. I want a perfect grade on that test. Right now, please.' All the students got really scared then. They all sensed something dark beneath his words.

"Mrs. Krick shook her head in disbelief. 'Now why would I do such a thing?'

"Mark Chester just smiled his most dangerous smile at her and said one more word. 'Blaze.'

"The class knew exactly what he meant and rushed out the door in an instant. Mrs. Krick started screaming, 'Where are you all going? Come back here right now!' But no one was listening. Soon, only Mark and Mrs. Krick were left in the room. She glared at Mark and yelled, 'Now look what you've done! You've frightened off my entire class! What do you have to say for yourself?'

"Mark just looked at her. He reached into his pocket and pulled out a cigarette lighter. He held it up and said, 'Flick!' Then he ignited it and said, 'Swish' as he threw the lighter onto the stack of exams on Mrs. Krick's desk. The papers burst into flames. Mark just grinned and whispered, 'Burn.' Mrs. Krick jumped away from her desk and out the door. The next moment, fire alarms were ringing and lights were flashing throughout the building. People

who were close enough to smell the smoke took off running for the nearest exits. The entire school was consumed in chaos and terror. Taylor, it was awful."

"What happened to Mark?" Taylor asked.

"He was expelled and arrested for arson. But believe me, he won't be missed. Everybody's glad that Mark Chester is finally gone."

All Taylor could say was, "Wow!"

"By the way," Kelly said, "I can't wait for your party! It's going to be so much fun!"

"I'm sure it will."

"Oh, it's getting rather late now and my parents are calling. So fussy . . . don't they think I'm responsible enough to go to bed on time? Oh, well. Goodnight, Taylor. I'll talk to you soon!"

As Taylor said goodbye to Kelly and lowered the phone, she thought of Mark Chester. *I wonder what's going to happen to Mark now.* As she reached for the dust cloth on the nightstand next to her, another thought dashed through her head. *Mark Chester . . . Chester . . . I wonder if he's related to Mr. Chester who owns the necklace.* Taylor rubbed the cloth over the nightstand until she saw her own reflection in the sparkling, clean surface.

Just then she realized something else. *Just one more day until my birthday,* Taylor thought as she dropped the rag. *Just one more day . . .*

Chapter Twenty-Seven

Taylor's eyes shot open and she cast aside her blankets. The dark stone walls of the castle were ominous in the night, and even the soft hisses of breath from her family were frightening. She arose from the pile of blankets and stepped from the chamber. Her bare feet hardly made a sound as they padded against the freezing floor. What was odd was Taylor knew neither where she was going nor why. She only knew she had to follow her heart. Something deep inside had awakened her and now it was guiding her past the sleeping villagers . . . through endless hallways . . . up a flight of stone steps . . . outside to the gardens . . .

Her legs carried her to the tower where she and Erik had glimpsed Chester when he stole the necklace from the countess. She rushed to the top of the tower. Only when her feet touched the stone landing did she halt. The wind whipped wildly through her clothes. The night was silent. Not a creature stirred in the forest. For a long while, Taylor stood confused. *Why did I come here?* But the next moment, she turned to face the sea and understood why her heart had led her there.

The countess stood on the sand far below the tower with the wind fluttering her pure white gown. She stood still. Her eyes were set upon the endless dark water. Then she made a movement . . . just one step. The shadowy sea washed up and covered her foot in darkness.

Taylor tried to cry out in terror, but her voice was lost under the crashing of the waves against the shore. She knew what the countess was doing. She flew down the staircase and out to the beach, but the woman was already up to her chest in the water.

"Countess, no! Please, come back! Come back!" Taylor cried through her tears.

The countess turned, but she only smiled. Her eyes were shining with a distant light. Slowly, she dipped her fingers into the sea. With perfect grace, she drew a ring around herself in the water. A glowing white flame appeared wherever her hand touched the surface until the countess was surrounded by white fire.

She then looked up at Taylor and whispered, "There shall come a time when you shall be glad of what I do now. I will not tell you why, for in due time you will find out for yourself. But go now from this place. Go now and never forget . . ."

"What must I not forget? Please, tell me!" Taylor begged.

But the countess said no more. Instead, she turned to the sea again. Taylor ran after her, but when her feet touched the water, the icy cold of the water cut through her skin like a knife. The sea around her feet suddenly grew glassy, and the surface froze over. Forced to draw back, Taylor's eyes filled with stinging tears. She watched as the woman walked farther and farther away until the water was over her head. Even when the countess disappeared, Taylor could still see the white light dancing beneath the waves.

Chapter Twenty-Eight

The sun's rays blazed through Taylor's window. She awoke suddenly, breathing hard. *The countess and the sea . . . what could it all mean?*

Taylor grimaced at the sun and closed the blinds. The light still managed to slip between a crack in the blinds and smile innocently at her. Taylor sighed and accepted that more sleep was out of her reach and went to take a shower. The water gently caressed her neck and shoulders and wound down her back in sparkling rivers. *What a nice way to begin the day and forget last night's terrors.*

After dressing in her best clothes, Taylor forced herself to abandon images of the dark sea and the countess. She skipped down the stairs and set her mind and body to the task of preparing the food for the party.

The aromatic scents wafting from the kitchen soon beckoned Amanda downstairs. The little girl decided to assist her sister, but, of course, the only thing she managed to accomplish was making a mess. At least the two of them had fun together throwing mashed potatoes across the kitchen. When Sarah came downstairs an hour later, she was furious and demanded the girls clean up the scattered food immediately. Alex only laughed when he finally made it to the kitchen.

The entire family pitched in preparing for the party. Taylor and Sarah prepared some of their favorite foods. Alex concocted a fabulous chicken dish topped off with spices, herbs, and a special sauce. Even Amanda did her share of the work by setting the table.

Erik revved the engine to life and backed his car down the driveway. He wiped away a small trickle of sweat that slid down the side of his face. His conscience raged against what he had done, but Erik fought back the guilt by thinking of the good his deed would bring. He thought of his mother hugging him, fully cured, and of Taylor's eyes filled with admiration. Those were the things he wished for, and he would get them. No matter the way. No matter the price. He would save his mother.

Only one more thing still tugged at the corners of his mind. He had the earrings from his mother and the necklace from Chester, but he still needed the bracelet, and he had no idea where to even begin searching for it. At that moment, a soft but dreadful voice whispered, *"What if the bracelet is gone? It was made centuries ago. Who knows if it still exists in its original form? What if it was melted down and reshaped? What if the emerald stones were removed and sold throughout the world? What will you do then?"*

Erik swallowed hard. He had already searched through countless magazines, infinite Internet sites, and all the jewelry stores in town, always looking for the emerald bracelet. He had seen hundreds of bracelets and thousands of different jewelry items containing emerald stones, but not one matched the bracelet from Taylor's dreams. With each passing day, Erik grew more and more worried. How long could his mother hold on? What if he ran out of time? What if he never found the bracelet?

Chapter Twenty-Nine

Vicky, Michael, and Kyle were the first ones at the party. They presented Taylor with a small, antique statue of a girl kneeling with her hands locked in prayer.

"Taylor, this is one of our family treasures," Vicky said as she handed Taylor the statue. "Your grandmother gave it to me on my fifteenth birthday. I hope it brings you as much happiness as it has brought me."

Vicky hugged her niece and kissed her cheek softly. Taylor accepted the gift and rubbed her fingers along the smooth bronze. She thanked Vicky, Michael, and Kyle profusely for the very special gift and placed the statue on the fireplace mantel for the time being.

Erik's family arrived next. To everyone's surprise, both of Erik's parents came with their son. Taylor was deeply touched when she saw that Erik's mother had made the effort to come despite her frail condition.

Erik's parents had never visited the Creekmore's house. They marveled at its beauty. Alex offered the pair a tour of the home, which they gladly accepted, and allowed themselves to be led away.

Kelly was the last to arrive. She explained that her parents had been working and couldn't drop her off any earlier. Taylor introduced her best friend to Erik and Kyle. When Kyle saw Kelly, he grinned and winked at Taylor. They all chatted in the living room until Erik's parents and Alex returned. Finally, they proceeded to the dining room.

When they had found their seats, Erik's father stood up and warmly congratulated Taylor on her fifteenth birthday. When he sat down, he handed Taylor a gift card from Barnes and Nobles. She thanked him graciously and stored the card safely in her pocket.

The air filled with the sounds of laughter, mirth, and chattering. Everyone thanked the generous hosts and murmured words of congratulations to the birthday girl. Kelly hugged her best friend so tightly that she could barely breath, and they laughed at jokes that Kyle told. Even Erik seemed to forget the terrible predicament facing his family and celebrated with the rest.

Later, everyone moved from the dining room to the home theater in the basement. The party's finale was watching a newly released movie. Taylor loved the movie, especially the ending. The movie ended when the hero and heroine walked out onto the deck of a cruise ship just as the sun was setting. They stood in silence for a long time, remembering their adventures. And then, when the sun had finally set and the sky was dark, the hero kissed the heroine and the credits rolled out.

After that, the three families and Kelly bid each other farewell and went their separate ways.

ౚ   ౚ   ౚ

As days turned to weeks, Erik tried with all his might to allay his fears. His mother was fading with every passing day. She now needed special injections to dispel her daily pain.

One day, the rage and terror in his soul was so great that Erik could no longer stand it. He had to get out of the house. Before he knew it, he found himself standing on the sidewalk in front of the house, letting the breeze comfort his soul. The wind wound between the houses and trees, carrying with it the sweet scent of roses and wild flowers. The shadows on the ground darkened as night swiftly approached.

Erik sat down wearily on a stone bench that stood near his house. He glanced first upon the sky, then upon the other homes in the neighborhood. Then, he closed his eyes and looked at nothing at all. But still, his thoughts burned with fire. As Erik sat there trying to calm his raging thoughts, he heard a soft whimpering and felt a light paw step on his shoe. Looking down, he saw Don looking up at him, tongue hanging out and panting happily. Erik's eyes slowly traveled from the dog's collar up the leash until they met Taylor's gaze.

"Taylor!" Erik cried softly.

She nodded and sat down beside him on the bench. Her lips curled into a smile. "Erik," she asked, "how's your mother? Is she any better? I was just thinking . . ."

But Erik never learned what Taylor was thinking because at that very moment a loud, wailing siren shattered the still night. Erik felt his heart tear as an ambulance roared into their subdivision, throwing up clouds of dust in its wake. Together, they watched in horror as the ambulance screeched to a stop and two men rushed into Erik's house with a stretcher.

Erik and Taylor ran to the house with Don trailing far behind them. When they entered, Erik headed upstairs shouting, "Mom! Dad!" As he reached his parents' room the paramedics were gently lifting his mother onto the stretcher. Erik rushed to his mother's side only to realize that she was unconscious. Erik's father stood in the middle of the room, his face washed white with fear and tears rolling down his cheeks.

Erik went over and put his arms around his father. Erik could feel his father's strength returning as he said, "Erik, I'm going in the ambulance with your mother. Please make sure the house is secured and meet me at the hospital."

His father rushed downstairs, barely glancing at Taylor as he made his way to the ambulance.

Erik and Taylor stood in silence. Both knew what the other thought. Instinctively, both reached out for the other's hand.

"Erik," Taylor finally asked, "do you want me to go to the hospital with you?" For a long moment, he just stood there motionless. Then, he gave the slightest shake of his head.

Taylor pulled Erik toward her and put her arms around him. Finally, Erik said, "I would love to have you come with me, but not tonight. Tomorrow, maybe. But tonight I must handle this on my own." He turned away from Taylor and rubbed tears from his eyes. Quietly, he whispered, "I need to lock up the house now. I'll see you later . . ."

"Okay," Taylor replied.

They quickly left the house. Erik ran to his car while Taylor stepped out onto the road with Don. Before Erik shut the car door, he took one last look at his friend. She stood alone now. The world around her had taken on a savage blend of shadows and darkness, raging in a silent war. But behind her, the setting sun's blood red rays blazed, casting everlasting sparks into the sky and fighting a losing battle against the coming darkness. Everywhere, Erik saw omens, foreshadowing, and the approach of a deadly night. Then he shut the door tightly and saw no more.

Taylor watched as the ambulance roared away into the night, followed closely by Erik's car. The night wind blew her clothes gently and brushed against her face. She stood there for a long time, long after the last traces of dust from the ambulance tires had settled. It was deep night when she finally turned to go home. Even Don, who was usually playful and happy, trailed sadly behind Taylor all the way home.

Chapter Thirty

An entire day had passed since the ambulance took Erik's mother to the hospital. Every time Taylor walked past the telephone, she wished Erik would call. But her hopes were in vain. *Perhaps I should call him myself,* she considered.

Taylor was home alone. Her father was at work, and Sarah had taken Amanda to her music lesson. To get her mind off her terrifying thoughts, she decided to clean up a little bit around the house. She started with the home theatre in the basement and worked her way up. Taylor finished with her own bedroom. Sighing, Taylor placed her hand on the doorknob and was about to leave when her gaze fell upon the bronze statue Vicky had given her. After the party had ended, Taylor had brought the statue up to her room.

She returned to her bed and lifted the statue in her hands, examining it closely. She hadn't given the praying girl any thought since her birthday party. Although the bronze had tarnished over the years, it was still beautiful. The smooth lines on the girl's face conveyed calm and tranquility. Her hands, pressed together in prayer, were graceful and well sculpted. Taylor ran her fingers along the statue's hands, admiring every detail.

That's when she felt it—a tiny, sharp prick on her finger. Taylor jerked her hand away and looked at the small wound. *Nothing serious,* she confirmed and returned her gaze to the statue. Wondering what pricked her, Taylor brought the statue to eye level and gave it an extra careful examination. It was only then that she noticed it. A small spring was jammed between the girl's folded hands. Taylor walked over to her desk and took one of her pens from the pencil cup. She brought it back to her bed and, taking great care not to damage the bronze, she pressed the spring with the tip of the pen.

She heard a creaking sound, and for one moment she was afraid that she had broken the statue. But the next moment was filled with immense curiosity when she saw what had really happened. The bottom of the statue had opened and something had fallen to the floor. Taylor's fingers began shaking as she reached for the object that lay at her feet. She nearly fainted as she placed it in the palm of her hand. Taylor was holding the bracelet from her dreams!

The sudden ringing of the telephone pulled Taylor back to reality. Her hand was still shaking when she picked up the phone. She heard Erik's weary voice. He spoke softly. "Taylor, she's dying. I'm losing her, Taylor. I don't . . ."

"Erik, I found the bracelet!" Taylor exclaimed, her thoughts racing fast and her heart pumping hard. "Oh, Erik . . . I found the bracelet!"

ɷ   ɷ   ɷ

An hour later, Taylor and Erik stood near the boy's dying mother in the hospital. The room was empty except for them and a nurse. Erik's mother lay unconscious. Erik and Taylor waited until the nurse left the room. In his fist, Erik clutched the emerald earrings. Taylor held a loose grip on the bracelet. They each held part of the necklace, and it joined them together as one. In a single, fluid motion, they placed the necklace on the woman's brow. Erik gave the earrings to Taylor, and she handed the bracelet to him. Taylor fastened the earrings tightly onto her ears and Erik pulled the bracelet over his hand and onto his wrist. The two joined their free hands and stood silently as they waited for the emeralds to work their magic.

Taylor watched Erik's mother carefully, but there was no change in her white complexion. *But we did everything right! Why is nothing happening?* Then it hit her. The words . . . the countess had spoken something and only then had the disease passed. But what had she said? Tears welled up in Taylor's eyes. How could she have forgotten? All their hope had been in vain. They had failed. Why couldn't she remember the words?

Suddenly, Taylor heard the now familiar voice of the spirit. "Do not fear," the spirit whispered in her head. "I shall help you. Tell Erik to repeat after you."

"Erik, repeat after me. Just trust me."

Taylor concentrated on the spirit's voice. It spoke words in an unfamiliar language, but she and Erik repeated them nonetheless. Together, they prayed for Erik's mother and for the passing of the evil that had descended upon her. With each word, the woman's skin regained more of its color and the shadowy feeling of death started to fade from the room.

As they said the ancient words, Taylor noticed a tiny flame, hardly noticeable but there nevertheless, sparked in the emerald stone of the necklace. The woman's labored breathing started to ease, and her heartbeat steadied. After what seemed like forever to the two young people, Erik's mother opened her eyes and smiled.

Chapter Thirty-One

The days that followed were a hazy blur of joyous memories to Taylor. After the doctors announced that Erik's mother was literally a medical miracle, their family returned home and the celebrations began. Erik invited Taylor to attend the prom with him. They spent the night dancing, laughing, and partying with their friends until the faculty chaperones had finally chased them out of the school. It was a great night, and Taylor slept through the entire next day.

Erik graduated summa cum laude, and at long last, the final commemoration of his mother's recovery arrived. As a thank you, Erik's family invited the Creekmores to join them on a cruise on a yacht. When they accepted, Erik convinced his parents to invite Vicky, Michael, and Kyle to join them, too.

When Taylor called Kelly to tell her about the cruise, Kelly begged her parents to let her go on vacation with her best friend. Kelly's parents agreed to purchase the ticket if the Creekmores were okay with Kelly joining them. Alex and Sarah were delighted to have Kelly accompany them, and the two girls were thrilled.

Now, Taylor, Erik, Kyle and Kelly sat together in chairs near the dock, waiting for the *Dream Line* to begin boarding passengers. Taylor glanced over at her parents and sister, who were looking over a pamphlet that described the tour. They would be visiting several countries. Taylor laid her head back on her crossed arms and smiled. *Exotic lands, here I come!*

"So," Erik asked, turning to Taylor, "are you ready for our big adventure?"

"You bet I am," she said. "I can hardly wait! I can't believe we're going to be sailing on a yacht! I mean, how much better could things get?"

Kelly squirmed in anticipation. "This is going to be awesome!"

"And don't forget," Amanda said, looking up from the pamphlet, "since there are only thirty passengers on this cruise, I should get lots of personal attention!"

"That's all you think about, Amanda. Getting attention," Taylor said, rolling her eyes.

"I care about other things too, you know! For example, I can't wait to cross the China Sea and explore the island of Thaifura. I wonder if there'll be any fun places to play there?"

"Oh, right," Taylor said. "I forgot. All you care about is getting attention and playing."

"Exactly . . . hey, wait a second!" Amanda exclaimed angrily. Taylor grinned and quickly made herself scarce.

Suddenly, a shrill whistle erupted from the *Dream Line*. A steward announced they were ready for passengers to board the ship. The four friends jumped up and ran over to their parents, who were standing close by. Kelly went with Taylor and her parents as they made their way up the plank to the *Dream Line's* deck.

Taylor gasped in awe at the amazing view from the railing. The *Dream Line* rocked gently in the water and Taylor, having not yet gotten her sea legs, started to feel a little sick. Although she wanted to watch the ship set sail, she decided that it would be a better idea to go below deck and get a little rest.

She made a beeline straight for her parents and asked them for the key to their room. Alex laughed and hugged his daughter around the middle. "Oh, come now, you don't want to miss the ceremony, do you?"

"Ceremony?" Taylor asked, immediately forgetting all about her nausea. She leaned over the railing again and saw a group of men carrying a large bottle of champagne towards the ship. Surprised, she asked, "Don't they only do that to brand new ships?"

"Exactly! This is the *Dream Line's* maiden voyage," Sarah answered.

Taylor groaned and stared up at the sky. The very last thing she wanted now was an untested ship. Swallowing hard, she watched as the men smashed the bottle against the bow of the ship.

Presently, she heard the roaring of the powerful engine as the yacht left the dock. Taylor took one last longing look at land before the *Dream Line* moved forward. On shore, people waved to the ship and yelled wishes for a safe voyage. Grinning wildly, Amanda cheered with the rest, bouncing up and down with excitement. Looking at her sister, Taylor sincerely wished she could have the same innocent enthusiasm, but since she boarded the ship, something in the very depths of her soul told her this cruise was a bad idea. For now, the most she could do was wave and celebrate with the others. She hoped with all her heart this would be a trip to always remember . . . in a good way, of course.

"Hey, what cabin are you staying in?" Kelly asked Taylor.

"Not the same one you're in, unfortunately. But we'll still see plenty of each other."

"Right. Bye, then. I'm feeling a bit sick right now and I think I should go to my cabin." Kelly swayed slightly and looked away from her best friend. Taylor smiled and turned away too. Like Kelly, she was beginning to feel very ill.

To relieve herself of the nausea, Taylor went down to her cabin. Sitting on the bed, she opened her purse and pulled out a green velvet pouch. Taylor glanced down to look at the emerald necklace, earrings and bracelet. Erik and his mother had given her the necklace and earrings as a special thank-you gift. Her fingers danced lightly over the jewelry. She didn't know why, but somehow, she felt she might very well need it before this trip was through. Besides, she had promised the countess she would keep the necklace with her always.

Well, at least there's one good thing about this trip, Taylor thought as she sat down at the dinner table with the others. *I have really good company.* Erik sat to her left and Kelly to her right. On the table before each of them lay a sparkling white plate and a beautiful set of silver cutlery. A napkin was placed on each plate, and a crystal goblet rested to the right of the napkin. Taylor twiddled her thumbs and looked around, wondering when their meal would arrive.

It was not long before three waiters, each dressed in a black and white uniform, swept over to the table. Each carried an enormous bowl of some exotic soup. Taylor hoped that the soup would be delicious. As soon as the soup bowls were placed on the table, she took off the lid of one bowl and took a deep whiff of the soup. The moment the scent reached her nose, she gave a great cough and dropped the steel lid. It rolled off the edge of the table and landed with a loud clatter on the floor.

Sarah looked over angrily at her daughter. "Taylor!" she exclaimed. "Pick up that lid right now and behave yourself. Eat what you get or leave the table this instant!"

Taylor looked away in embarrassment and dipped her spoon into the soup. The soup was a murky brown liquid. Pieces of what she sincerely hoped was meat drifted slowly among the other ingredients, including carrots, broccoli, and little pieces of parsley. She motioned for Erik and Kelly to lean closer and whispered softly, "I have an odd feeling that the spoon is going to taste better than the meal."

Erik and Kelly grinned and dove wholeheartedly into the soup. *Some people will eat anything,* thought Taylor.

"This soup's . . . really . . . good," Kelly said between mouthfuls. "Go on . . . try some."

Taking the utmost caution, Taylor brought her spoon up to her lips. Giving the foul mixture one last sniff, she allowed the liquid to trickle into her mouth. Without a single pause, she swallowed and waited for the flavor to settle in. It was delicious! Taylor eagerly consumed the rest of her soup. She even asked for a second helping.

After Kelly and Taylor finished their meals, they decided to find another table where they could just sit together and talk without being surrounded by lots of other people.

Walking side by side, Kelly and Taylor set out to find a table where they could be alone. But they hadn't gone very far when Amanda popped up out of nowhere and stood in front of the girls, blocking their path. Taylor sighed, took her sister by the shoulders, and steered her away from Kelly.

"What are you doing here? Why aren't you with Mom and Dad?" Taylor whispered angrily.

"Because you're more fun and because I want to play!"

"Play? Are you insane? This is supposed to be a vacation for both of us, not just you! And I'm not spending my vacation playing with you. That's torture, not fun!"

Amanda's eyes grew very watery and she looked like she was about to cry. She wailed, "But I . . . want . . . to!"

Oh, dear, Taylor thought. She knew that if Amanda cried, their parents would force her to play with her younger sister anyway. So she did the only thing she could.

"How would you like to hang around with me and Kelly for a little bit?" Taylor said. "That way, you get to have fun, and I don't have to play."

Taylor knew Kelly probably wouldn't like the idea of keeping Amanda entertained throughout the whole trip, but there wasn't any other choice. At least, not for now.

"Okay!" Amanda shouted happily. She ran over to Kelly and pulled on her arm. "Lets go have some fun! We're going to have a great vacation!"

"We?" Kelly asked, looking astonished. "If we refers to Taylor and me, then fine. If you're counting yourself in it, then forget it. This is our vacation! Go play with some other kids."

"Calm down, Kelly," Taylor said, seeing Amanda's eyes get watery again. "I don't see a problem with letting Amanda hang out with us. After all, this is a vacation. Let's just go find a table. I'm sure she won't bother us too much." But when Amanda went into a monologue about playing, Taylor wasn't so sure anymore. *Poor Kelly. And she thought this would be a nice, quiet vacation.* She smiled and shook her head.

∾ ∾ ∾

The next few days swept by swiftly and perfectly. Taylor, Erik, Kyle, Kelly, and even Amanda were almost constantly in each other's company and had a swell time together.

On the morning of their fourth day, the captain announced that they were approaching their first destination. They were about to arrive on a small island far out in the Pacific Ocean where they would partake in the island's most famous attraction. What that attraction was, however, was a mystery. It was one of the exciting adventures the tour line had promised.

When they disembarked, Taylor and her friends made their way into the island's port city. As Taylor walked about the city, she began to have an eerie feeling about this mystery attraction.

Sharks. Lots and lots of sharks. Every window of every shop in the city was decorated with posters of ferocious looking sharks. It seemed every sign and poster made the appeal "Dive with your Worst Nightmare!" or "Have Fun in the Jaws of the Terror of the Sea!" Some passengers found these images inviting, but Taylor took care to stay as far away from them as possible.

Although she managed to evade every poster, avoiding the real thing proved impossible. The day after they landed on the island, all of the passengers were herded to a vast dock full of ships of every size and shape. Although the sun sparkled pleasantly on the clear water, Taylor was in no mood for a show of beauty. The only thing she wanted was to get back to the *Dream Line* as fast as she could. Swallowing hard, she craned her neck to see what was happening at the front of the crowd.

"Well, here we are," a cheerful man at the front of the tour group announced. Taylor stood in the back alone, glancing around fearfully. Her friends, on the other hand, were all fighting for a spot in the front. Unlike her, they were quite eager to partake in the famous attraction, whatever it happened to be. Taylor, on the other hand, only wished for the entire expedition to be over. Much to her dismay, it was only beginning.

The man in the front cleared his throat and continued. "I'll be your guide through the great reef and beyond!" he exclaimed. *Beyond what?* Taylor wondered before he went on. "Today, we will go swimming among the many wonderful and mysterious fish that live in the waters surrounding our island. Now, doesn't that sound like fun?"

No, Taylor mentally replied as she followed the others to a dressing room. The men went one way, and the women went another. Upon entering the dressing room, she found an attendant waiting to help the ladies select wet suits for scuba diving. A jolt of fear ran through Taylor as she donned the suit with the attendant's help and returned outside to join the rest of the group.

The tourists all waited together until everyone was ready. Then, the cheerful guide led them to a small excursion boat. They were instructed to board, where they would be told exactly what awaited them. With growing apprehension, Taylor joined the others onboard and soon the boat was sailing over a vast, brilliantly colored coral reef.

The boat suddenly splashed to a stop and everyone became silent. Only the gentle splash of shimmering waves against the hull could be heard. The man who served as their tour guide flipped himself over the side of the boat and waved his hands for them to follow.

"Just jump over the side and follow me," he said. "Don't worry. Follow my lead and everything will be absolutely fine!" He submerged himself in the water and was gone.

Taylor swallowed hard as she jumped over the edge of the boat. Although she could not feel the wetness of the waves through her wetsuit, she still felt a chill in her blood as she lowered her head beneath the water. Taylor was slightly relieved when she saw the others all around her, some looking as frightened as she felt. The majority of the tourists, however, looked around excitedly, waiting for something to happen. It did not take long for their wish to become a reality.

As soon as they swam close to the coral reef, an enormous multitude of various fish, each blazing like a rainbow, burst toward them. Even Taylor gasped in wonder at the amazing sight. The small fish were soon joined by larger fish, all swimming in perfect harmony and at peace with the world. Before long, Taylor was enjoying herself completely. She laughed and wondered how she could have ever thought they would be doing something dangerous. This was pure bliss . . . pure contentment . . . pure . . . joy.

That's when she saw it. A single fish longer than she was tall flashed past her. The fish's scales flared like a flame, and its fluid movements hypnotized the girl. Never had she seen such an amazing creature! She turned and swam after it, never losing sight of the fish. On and on the fish swam, and for a long time, Taylor followed. When her legs had nearly given out, the burning fish vanished without a trace. Taylor looked all around, but the fish was nowhere to be found. She heaved a sigh and turned around to join the group of tourists.

But all she saw was coral and water. Deep, dark, empty water. With a gasp, Taylor realized what she had done. By following the fish, she had gotten separated from the others. She did not see a single sign of the tour group. Fear gripped Taylor as she glanced around in horror. *Where am I? What should I do?* she wondered. *Well, at least there aren't any dangerous creatures around here.*

Or so she thought. Taylor noticed something odd. Or rather, she felt more than saw the dark blade streaking through the water beneath her. The sea around her churned and the dark shape below halted, its nostrils dilating to locate the source of her scent. With a flash of dagger-like teeth, the dark shape formed into a monstrous shark. The creature clamped its jaws and hurdled like a torpedo at the young diver.

Taylor's heart nearly froze as she watched the shark fling itself at her. Doing the only thing she could think of, she thrashed her legs in an attempt to swim away. Using a piece of outstretched coral as a springboard, she thrust herself forward and away from the mouth of the beast. The shark's jaws missed her by a single inch, but the distance was soon made up as the monster turned and attempted another bite. Taylor's heart squeezed in terror and she tried to swim away again. But her legs were too tired after the vigorous fish chase and could not propel her any further. Realizing that this was the end, Taylor turned to face the shark head on. *I'd rather die looking death in the face than hiding from my fate,* she concluded desperately and readied herself for the worst.

It never came. Suddenly, a screech echoed from behind, below, and all around Taylor. It was a single note of life, safety, and perhaps even of love. The shark halted and thrashed its tail, sniffing again to discern the position of its enemy.

Suddenly, dolphins poured in from everywhere. One dolphin swam to Taylor. It pushed its soft nose against her hand and looped its curved fin beneath her arm. Understanding what the dolphin wanted her to do, Taylor gripped its fin with all her might and swung her other arm over the dolphin's side. She looked over at the shark and found it was surrounded by a large group of dolphins. The dolphin she was holding on to sped off. Taylor closed her eyes, not wanting to see what might happen next.

It was not until the dolphin cleared the surface that Taylor dared to open her eyes. Far ahead, she saw a large mound and tiny speck hovering above the water. She assumed that the mound was the island and the speck was the boat. The dolphin's streamlined body slipped beneath the waves again for a second before surfacing again. Taylor and the dolphin became one as their bodies darted beneath the waves and rose again, over and over. Soon, many more dolphins joined them. They soared over the ocean like great birds from the sea, crashing into the ocean with sheets of spray flailing out on all sides. Only Taylor's dolphin kept a straight path on the surface while the others jumped around them.

The other panic-stricken tourists were waiting for Taylor when she got back to the boat. Her parents and sister were first in line to hug and cry over her. They informed her that many of them believed her lost. Apologizing, the tour guide explained that the area he led them through was typically free from sharks, and the ones they normally saw on the tour were no threat to humans.

"Apparently," he commented, "the one you met had strayed into these waters. Of course, this would never have happened if you had stayed with the others."

Taylor knew it had been foolish of her to get separated from the others. *But if I had stayed with the group,* Taylor thought, *I would have never met the dolphins.* She smiled as she watched the dolphins leaping away into the blue sea. *I guess some things are just worth breaking the rules for . . .*

∾ ∾ ∾

The following day, just when they were about to reach their next destination, the passengers were told they would soon have the pleasure of watching an elephant polo match. *Elephant polo?* Taylor wondered as she stood on the deck, eagerly watching the sailors prepare to dock the ship.

Erik and Kyle leaned against the railing to Taylor's left, talking quietly to one another. On her other side, Kelly's eyes were closed and her chin rested on the rail. Only Amanda appeared as excited as Taylor. Her eyes searched out every detail of the large hulk of land that was quickly coming forth to meet the ship. Once or twice, Taylor had to grab hold of the girl's shirt to stop her from falling over the railing. She could understand Amanda's eagerness. Had she been younger, she would have done the same.

Half an hour later, the passengers of the *Dream Line* walked down the plank and joined the bustling crowds on the island of Thaifura. The streets were so densely packed that the families had a hard time keeping up with each other in the crowds. Finally, Sarah suggested that they should stay at a café until the foot traffic died down some. Then, they could all go sightseeing together. Everyone agreed that it was a marvelous idea and a pleasant way to pass the time.

Taylor and her friends strode through the doorway of The China Palace, a quaint little café by the ocean. They were absolutely astonished by the café. Everything inside was made to look like an old-world marketplace. Tiny wooden chairs stood around a hand carved table near the counter, which was decorated by an exquisite carving of the ocean and palm trees. The walls were adorned with seashell wallpaper, and the carpet was a stunning sky blue. The woman standing behind the counter smiled sweetly and welcomed them to the café. After being seated near the window, they ordered drinks and waited for the crowds to pass.

Half an hour later, the families left The China Palace and began to explore the seaport village. Taylor and Kelly particularly enjoyed the various origami figures and expertly woven baskets and clothing that the old women in the streets were selling. The two boys preferred the sports shop near the village square. Amanda, who went with her older sister and Kelly, squealed every time they passed a toy and had to be dragged away by Taylor and Kelly. Their parents spent the rest of the day at a coffee shop, drinking coffee and cappuccino and catching up on news. In the evening, they all met at the village square and walked together to the polo field where the match would be held.

But what is elephant polo? Taylor asked herself again.

The stadium was already crowded with locals and tourists, all holding flags or wearing shirts displaying their favorite team's name. Taylor made a quick note of the names. Many of the shirts proclaimed "Raiders." However, there were also a few labeled "Steel Tusks." *Apparently, the Raiders are favored to win this match.* As they made their way around the stadium grounds, Taylor noticed a sign that explained how elephant polo was played. It read:

THE RULES OF ELEPHANT POLO

1. The game is played by two teams with four players each using a standard size polo ball.
2. The game consists of two 10-minute periods of playing time with an interval of 15 minutes. Play starts and stops at the sound of the referee's whistle.
3. The pitch is 140 x 70 meters. It is marked with a centerline, a circle with a radius of 15 meters in the center of the field, and a semi-circle with a radius of 30 meters measured from the center of the goal line at either end of the pitch. Elephants and ends are changed at half time.

Suddenly, the sound of a trumpet shattered the evening air, signaling the start of the match. Eight elephants ambled slowly onto the field, four wearing black and red and four adorned in silver. The crowds gave a mighty roar

when the players ran out onto the field shortly after their elephants. Each player mounted his elephant and the referee, who was wearing neither black nor red nor silver, but a gold colored robe, emerged with a polo ball. One elephant from each team strode forth to the marked circle in the center of the field, and a hush fell over the crowd. All eyes were now on the referee as he pulled back his hand and sent the ball sailing into the circle where the elephants and the men were waiting. In a single, fluid motion, both men raised their polo sticks and brought them down in two powerful swings. The man on the black and red elephant struck the ball and sent it flying toward the opposing team's semi-circle.

The crowd erupted with noise, but Taylor wasn't even paying attention to whether it was friendly or not. Her eyes were focused solely on the elephants and the men. She watched as the ball went up and down the field a few times before a man on a silver-clothed elephant scored a goal.

"The Steel Tusks just scored the first goal of the match!" the announcer exclaimed. "But will it be enough to claim the title of champion?"

From that point on, the game took on such a fast pace that Taylor had trouble keeping up. Never had she known elephants to move as swiftly as those on the field. Although the Steel Tusks scored the first goal, the Raiders quickly made it obvious why they were favorites. The Raiders played so fast and fierce that the grass beneath their elephant's legs was torn up in places. They not only scored a goal after two more minutes of play, but they also prevented the Steel Tusks from even touching the ball. By half time, the crowd was hoarse from screaming and the score was tied.

After a fifteen-minute intermission, the elephants were back on the field and ready to go. The crowd was silent again as the referee threw the ball into play, but when the Raider in the center hit the ball toward the Silver Tusks' goal once more, the crows erupted.

Three of the Raiders circled three of the Silver Tusks to stop them from coming near the ball. Meanwhile, the Raider and Silver Tusk who had started in the circle were chasing after the polo ball, each trying to score the winning goal for his team. Neck and neck, the two elephants raced to the ball, each as determined as the other to get there first. The Raider raised his polo stick high in the air and swung down at the ball. A swish. A hit. The soaring of a ball. The soft landing of a polo ball in the goal. The silence before a victory.

Then, in a single moment, the crowd exploded and fans rushed from the sidelines onto the field, Taylor among them, to congratulate the Raiders on their win. Although Taylor knew nothing about the sport or the players, she took great joy in shouting "Congratulations!" along with everyone else.

The fans partied through the night. Taylor and her friends enjoyed the festivities until it was time to return to the ship. As they walked back to the dock, Taylor reflected on the day's activities and decided that their vacation was definitely taking a turn for the better.

Chapter Thirty-Two

Taylor sat in her cabin, brushing her long hair. It was the morning after the elephant polo game and she felt tired, but not tired enough to stay in her room. As soon as she combed her hair and changed, she would find her friends and they would come up with something interesting to do. With this happy thought in mind, Taylor turned to gaze at her reflection in the mirror . . . but then screamed in terror and whirled away, her heart beating wildly. Instead of seeing her face in the mirror, Taylor had seen the back of her head. Everything in the mirror was facing backwards. Very slowly, she turned back to the mirror, but nothing had changed. She still did not see her face.

Puzzled, Taylor placed her palm on the glass. Strangely, the back of her hand was reflected in the mirror. She then turned her hand so the back was pressed against the mirror. This time, her palm was reflected in the glass.

It seems, she thought, *that this mirror reflects the opposite side of whatever appears in it.*

"Taylor . . ." cried a distant voice.

Remembering her friends, she glanced up at the clock. To her horror, she saw that the clock was going backwards! The hands of the clock were spinning wildly out of control! The lights overhead flickered suddenly and died. The room was thrown into complete darkness. Taylor drew in a deep breath and turned toward the mirror again.

"Taylor . . ."

Her mouth opened in a wordless scream as human faces appeared in the mirror. They seemed to be surrounded by white flames that flickered just beyond the glass surface of the mirror.

"Taylor . . ."

The faces were made of shining, billowing clouds of smoke. Their empty eyes glowed with a distant, unearthly light. The room was silent, yet Taylor could hear soft breathing. It filled the room, and the girl started to grow cold.

"Taylor . . ."

Terrified, Taylor fled from the cabin and ran down the hall to find her friends.

The sun had long since set, leaving the world in shadows. The weather was still and windless. The ocean was calm like a flat mirror. And yet, Taylor could not help but feel there was something dark lurking beneath the surface of the sea as she stood with her father upon the deck. Suddenly, one of the sailors yelled, "Fire at sea! Fire at sea!"

The night was very dark. The moon had not yet risen, and it was difficult to make out anything, even if it was only a few steps away. It was impossible for light to reflect off the water.

And yet, about a mile from the ship, a brilliant white flame glowed beneath the surface of the sea.

"How strange!" Alex commented. "But I suppose there are many things in nature that cannot be explained."

Suddenly, Taylor heard a sigh come from one of the other people on deck. Turning around, she saw that the ship's captain had come out onto the deck to enjoy the fresh air. She assumed that another member of the crew had taken over the ship's controls. When the captain overheard what Alex said, he shook his head and said, "Still, I think an explanation can be found for everything. The only problem is finding those explanations. Everything that we claim is supernatural is only said to be so because of our ignorance. Once we can explain it, it is no longer considered supernatural."

"Well, there is one of those supernatural things," Alex countered. "Can you explain that?"

A woman standing near the two men turned and said, "This isn't the first time I've seen one of those white flames. They often appear above graves. I've heard many tales about fires such as this one."

Alex looked puzzled. "Do you think these flames are the spirits of the dead?"

"Could be," she replied.

"Ha! That's what you say. The fires can't be spirits because there is an explanation for them, too. The white fire that we're looking at has a perfectly logical explanation and has nothing to do with spirits. This phenomenon can be repeated in any place," the captain said with a smirk. "It is only a phosphoric production of gases that occurs when living things decompose. The gases arise from either earth or swamp and burn when they touch air. I suppose they simply encountered a stray air bubble in the water."

Alex shook his head but said nothing.

While the captain laughed, the woman only looked on in silence. There was a strange glow on her face and her dress fluttered softly, although there was no wind. As she retreated to the shadowy corners of the ship, she whispered, "That's what you think, captain."

Meanwhile, the ship had continued its voyage and had now approached the flame. Only two hundred feet separated the ship from the white fire.

"Get ready to halt the ship," the captain ordered. "Draw as near as possible without actually touching the flame. I want to take a look at it."

Suddenly, the fire began to sink into the depths of the ocean as if it understood the captain's command. When the *Dream Line* came to a complete stop, the flame reemerged on the opposite side of the ship.

"Now we'll see what this flame really is," the captain said. "Call the scuba diver!"

The diver pushed his way through the crowd of people and stood before the captain. "Yes, sir," he said. "You called for me?"

"Yes. Do you see that white flame? What do you suppose it is?"

"Well, sir, I'm not sure. I would have to get closer to the fire to really tell what it is."

The captain nodded to the man and said, "Then I want you to dive and look at the flame underwater." The passengers and crew waited with baited breath as the diver donned his scuba gear and gracefully splashed into the sea.

The water near the fire was so cold that the parts nearest the flame were solid ice. The diver circled around the sphere of light, but he couldn't make out what it was. He had never seen such a thing. When he neared the light, he reached out and touched the white fire. Amazingly, it did not burn him. But then, suddenly, the fire began to descend into the darkness of the sea. Soon, the light was barely noticeable, and then it vanished entirely from sight. The diver returned to the ship and climbed up on the deck.

"I don't . . . I can't . . . that fire! It was incredible! When I neared it, something seemed to push me away. I thought I heard voices beneath the water, but I'm not sure. I touched it, but it didn't burn me. Captain, I really can't explain it. I've never seen anything like it."

"I know all of this is very mysterious, but somehow, I feel as if I've seen this somewhere before," Taylor said quietly to her father.

Suddenly, the captain yelled, "My God!"

"What is it?" Alex asked, turning.

"Look! There!" the captain said, pointing to where the fire had been.

They all turned to gaze at the sea. The white fire had risen to the surface again, but this time it was larger. Water poured off in torrents as the sphere rose from the sea and hovered in midair. The fire churned and slowly transformed into a human shape.

Long pearly curls cascaded down to the shoulders of a white woman who had risen from the black sea. She wore a long gown that billowed in a nonexistent wind. The bright light in her eyes could be seen from the ship, although it was two hundred feet away.

As Taylor watched, confused and scared, she remembered the countess' words from a forgotten dream. *There shall come a time when you shall be glad of what I do now. I will not tell you why, for in due time you will find out for yourself. But go now from this place. Go now and never forget . . . never forget . . . never forget.*

In that instance, Taylor realized who the woman was. The woman in the sea was the spirit of the countess. Taylor had not forgotten, but she did not understand. *Why has the countess returned now?*

The passengers on the deck gave another cry as the white woman in the sea turned into fire once again and slipped beneath the water into the depths of the ocean.

Silence settled over the ship while the passengers mused over what they had seen. But only Taylor knew the truth . . . the countess had returned.

Chapter Thirty-Three

The thunderous roar of the *Dream Line*'s engine shattered the morning calm. Taylor rubbed sleep from her eyes and glanced over at Amanda. Her sister still lay in the bed next to her, her chest rising and falling slowly as she slept. She knew that her parents lay peacefully in the cabin next door. Taylor tiptoed out of the cabin, being careful not to awaken Amanda, and crept up the stairs leading to the deck.

The gentle dawn wind blew through her hair. The new sun cast shimmering light across the water, and it reflected from the ocean to Taylor's heart. She closed her eyes and stood still, resting her arms against the railing and enjoying the morning breeze. It was not long before Kelly joined her friend. They stood in silence and admired the ocean in the early dawn. A few minutes later, Erik and Kyle joined them as well. They leaned against the rail and watched the sea with eager eyes. For a long time, they were the only ones on deck, and the thrilling sound of silence in the face of a new day filled them with joy.

But their peace was short-lived. Soon, they heard another pair of feet. The newcomer thundered up the stairs and ran across the deck to the rail on the other side of the ship. At first, the person did not bother them, but finally a voice spoke up. "Um . . . Taylor . . . everyone . . . I think that we may have a small problem . . ."

Recognizing Amanda's voice, Taylor turned around to see what the problem was. What she saw made her mouth drop open.

A solid wall of darkness filled the sky behind the ship. An infinite collection of swirling black clouds filled the sky with shadows and made even the rising sun seem like a tiny pinprick against the ultimate nightfall. Taylor and her friends crowded around Amanda. The shadows seemed to eat away at the sky. Kelly was the first to speak, her voice quivering. "I've never seen anything like it. What do you think it is?"

Erik, Kyle, and Taylor all shook their heads, but Amanda had a theory. "The only thing that is even close to that would be a typhoon," she said. "I saw it once on the Weather Channel. The way those clouds all swirl and blend together to look like one vast cloud indicates powerful wind, and the mass of darkness signifies a powerful storm."

"A typhoon?" Kelly squeaked. "But we're in the middle of an ocean! I heard the captain say our next destination is four days away. There's no way we'll make it to port in time, and I don't think this ship can stand up against such a storm!"

"If the storm hits this ship," Amanda said, "we'll probably capsize."

The five friends exchanged looks of intense fear. Taylor couldn't believe that just two nights ago she had watched a game of elephant polo and everything had been fine. Now they were on the verge of a devastating collision with nature. She looked back at the sea and her eyes filled with tears of terror as she watched the dark, raging waters that approached in the wake of the typhoon.

Kyle cleared his throat and said, "Maybe we should go see the captain. He might already have a plan for getting us through this."

"But what can he do? The captain can't stop a typhoon," Taylor said sadly.

"But he's an experienced sailor. I'm sure he's been through many storms at sea," said Erik.

Luckily, they caught the captain talking to a member of the crew on the lower deck. They learned that the *Dream Line* was already sailing on a direct course to a nearby island. The captain also confirmed their fears of a typhoon, and he added that the rest of the cruise would have to wait until the storm passed and the waters were safe again.

The five friends left even more worried than before. After announcing the terrible news to their families, they returned to the deck and watched as a tiny hill of land in the distance grew nearer. They felt helpless as angry waves churned and raged in the sea below.

An hour later, the ship came to a stop at the small port city of Flamesdale, the only city on the little island of Ash. As Taylor descended down the walkway to the city below, she found herself wondering about the origin of the island's name. *Ash . . . what a strange name for an island.*

The passengers of the *Dream Line* were taken to Volcanus, the only hotel in the city. They all spent a fitful night, wondering what would become of them and the ship. The next morning, some of the passengers decided to explore the island to take their minds off the storm.

The landscape outside the city was completely desolate. Jagged rocks jutted from the bare ground. The island was comprised of a series of ragged cliffs overlooking the sea.

Taylor followed the others as they treaded through the rocky terrain. She wondered where they were going. Suddenly, the stones beneath her feet started to clatter and leap off the ground. She let out a cry, and the others turned to see what the trouble was. But before they could move, the ground lurched and everyone toppled to the ground. The earth let loose a fearsome howl that was followed by a low grumble. The ground cracked and shattered into pieces around them as repeated tremors shook the earth. Taylor followed the largest crack with her eyes to its source, and she gasped at what she saw.

A plume of flames showered a vast mountain to the west. Rivers of blazing rock spiraled down its sides in great torrents. Embers and ashes flew from the mountain's peak and covered all of the passengers. *So that's why it's called Ash Island,* Taylor had time to realize before a great rush of thick black clouds obscured her vision and everything blended into darkness.

Taylor was jolted back into consciousness by the gentle slap of rain on her face. She dug her elbows into the ground and pushed herself to a sitting position. Not too far from her, the other passengers were standing up and dusting soot from their clothes. Kyle helped Kelly to her feet and Erik squatted nearby, rubbing ash between his fingers. Amanda lay flat on the ground, staring up at the sky. Taylor smiled at her and stood up.

A sudden flash of lightning caused Taylor to jump. She glanced seaward and saw the *Dream Line* bobbing like a toy boat as enormous waves pounded against its hull. She took a single step and ash swirled around her feet and rose around her in billowing clouds. Another flash of lightning and an explosion of thunder sent the passengers hurrying back to the hotel Volcanus. As she ran with the rest, she thanked God that the volcano had only given off a single, tiny eruption. Or so she thought . . .

Once everyone had arrived safely at the hotel, all the passengers gathered in the lobby for an emergency meeting. The captain of the *Dream Line* stood solemnly at the front, facing the crowd. Taylor squeezed into the front row and listened carefully to every word that was said.

The captain heaved a great sigh and began, "Folks, we have a choice to make and it may very well be a decision between life and death. I want all of you to understand our present predicament before making your final choice.

"As all of you know, a typhoon now rages outside the walls of this room. I have heard stories on the news that never before has such a monster storm been witnessed. This typhoon is the most deadly and intense storm to ever be recorded. Many researchers even believe that such a storm deserves to be in a category all on its own. *Typhoon* could not even begin to describe it. And it is because of this storm that we were forced to land on this island in an attempt to save our lives.

"However, you must notice that I say *attempt* and not *success*. That is because this was indeed an attempt, and a futile one at that. The island we have landed on is a volcanic island previously believed to be extinct. But now, after one thousand years of being dormant, the volcano on this island has resumed activity. The eruption you witnessed today was merely a tiny spark from its depths. According to the seismic monitors that constantly chart volcanic activity, the volcano is due to erupt within the next day. The eruption will be unlike any that has ever been experienced. It is predicted that this entire island will dissolve in a sudden explosion of flame and ash, never to be seen again.

"Therefore, we have a choice to make. We can either stay on this island or we can return to the ship and attempt to ride out the storm. If you choose to return to the ship, I assure you as captain I will do everything within my power to get the ship safely through the storm. If you choose to stay on the island, I can give you no guarantees. Normally, the captain would make this decision for you, but since all of our lives are at risk, I feel it is only right for you to participate in the decision. Because I am a ship's captain, I'm naturally drawn to the sea. However, please know that I will fully support whatever decision you make. I can only hope that the choice you make is the right one."

The captain fell into a chair and waited for the passengers to come to a consensus. His eyes sparkled as they scanned over the whispering crowd. Taylor stood still, her heart thundering in her chest. *This is insane! We're supposed to choose between a typhoon and a volcano!* Her mind raced madly as she tried to decide which option ensured the greatest probability of survival.

She heard the adults arguing around her. She saw them shaking their heads in confusion and one young woman crying, covering her face with her hands. She felt a tremor run through the crowd as they shouted and cried in helpless agony. Taylor knew kids were supposed to be seen and not heard, but now was the time to break that rule. She had to help the adults make a decision.

Everything around her drew together into a swirling mass of fire, ice, flames and waves. Then the world went pure white, neither fire nor ice, but something more. Pure serenity and bliss. Nothing more. . .

The words passed from her lips before she knew she had said them. Later, she reflected back on this moment and remembered that someone else had spoken the words for her. She was glad that the spirit she had first met at the hospital had come to help her then. But for now, she only spoke as she knew how.

"To the sea . . ." the spirit said, but its words passed through Taylor's lips in her own voice. Taylor wasn't sure she had heard the familiar voice until the spirit spoke again. "To the sea . . ."

The entire crowd turned to face her as she walked over and stood beside the captain. She turned to the crowd and said, "Everyone, I believe we should take our chances at sea."

The captain smiled and nodded his approval. Taylor looked upon the other passengers, awaiting their choice. She heard them argue that to go to the ocean would result in definite drowning, whereas staying on the island could possibly save their lives. The volcano may not erupt at all, and they could happily spend the rest of their vacation in a hotel. Just as Taylor was certain they were doomed to die on the tiny island, Erik stepped out of the crowd and raised his voice to be heard.

"I heard everyone talking about staying on the island. I just want to point out that we've already experienced the first eruption from the volcano. To me, that guarantees the coming of more. Therefore, I agree with the captain and Taylor. I think our chances are better at sea."

Erik smiled at Taylor, and he grabbed her hand and held it tight. She felt a single tear slide down her face. It slid from her cheek and seemed to hang in midair for a second before landing on their hands. *At least I'm not alone.* But Erik was not the only one to join her. In another instant, Kelly was up before the passengers.

"I agree with Erik and would also like to add one thing. This island is so tiny that a volcanic eruption would consume all the land. There would be no place to run or hide. In the sea, you can always jump into the water if the ship capsizes. There is no such hope on land, especially if you are far inland. And even on the coast, a jump from the seaside cliffs would be deadly." She too came to stand beside Taylor. Kelly took Taylor's other hand and squeezed it tight.

Kyle ran up to claim the spotlight next. "What they have said is true. And, at any rate, I would rather side with this man who knows how to pilot his way through any predicament at sea than risk the uncertainty of remaining on this island. The captain has shown us that he is a leader we can follow. He has already done much to ensure panic does not spread. Notice that we do not stand here in utter alarm. There is calm among us because of the captain. Also, I truly believe my friends are right. Like them, I choose the path of the sea." Kyle walked over beside Kelly and took her free hand.

There was a long silence in the crowd. The captain and the four friends stood against the rest. Though the odds were against them, they stood their ground and waited patiently for the final decision. For a very long moment, no one moved or spoke. Finally, after what seemed to be an eternity, Amanda squeezed from the mass of people and stood between the two groups.

"Tell me, does this arguing help us escape from anything?" She turned to the crowd who favored the island. "Do you think you're doing anyone any good by staying on an island with a volcano that's about to erupt? Don't you realize that there is only one path to take?"

She moved over to stand beside the captain. Her voice quivered slightly as she said, "My parents say that water represents purity and life, while fire burns and destroys. Water is the life of the earth. Fire can only destroy you, but water can save you. I . . . I know my path. What will yours be?"

The entire room was silent as every pair of eyes rested upon the girl. The youngest and seemingly most foolhardy of them all now proved to be the most clever and true. By age she was young, but her thoughts were ancient. She might have the fault of loving to play, but that was a small price to pay for courage. Yet, even after her speech, there were doubters. The passengers burst into loud conversation. Above all were heard the voices of the kids' worried parents.

"But they're just kids! Are we really sure that they know what they're talking about?"

"They're kids who are right, though. Water would be safer."

"And the captain does know what he's doing . . ."

"It's the best idea we have, so onwards with it, I say!"

And then, without another word, the passengers all moved over to the side of the captain and there they all stood, waiting for the words that would seal their fate. *Way to go Amanda!* Taylor thought as she watched the captain rise and announce their next action.

"To the sea, then, we shall go. I urge you all to prepare your bags now. I myself shall tend to the *Dream Line*, along with my crew. We set sail this evening." As the captain headed for the exit, he passed by Amanda and ruffled her hair. Bending down so that no one else could hear, he whispered, "Thank you."

The passengers, as well as some of the residents of the island, were back on the ship before nightfall. They all remained on the deck and watched the tiny island grow smaller and smaller until it finally vanished. A constant drizzle of rain poured onto the ship as it sailed toward the open sea. They knew they would face the full force of the storm on the following day, so they enjoyed the deck while it was still possible. On this night, only the soft lights built into the ship lit the deck. There was not a single star in the sky.

Taylor sat on the deck with her parents for a little while before finally retiring to her room. She found Amanda in the room, jumping happily on her sister's bed. After shooing her sister away, Taylor fell on the bed and gave a deep sigh. *Well, at least I don't see how things could get any worse than this.*

After a few minutes, Taylor stood up from the bed again and leaned against her nightstand. She brushed her hand over the flat top and simply enjoyed the cool, smooth feeling of the stand's surface. When her hand slipped from the surface onto the top drawer's handle, she pulled it open. But when she looked down into the drawer, she gasped. She screamed and ran outside to call for help. However, it was not what she saw that had frightened her. Instead, it was what she did not see.

Erik met her in the hall. "Taylor, calm down! What happened?"

"The emerald jewelry is gone!"

Chapter Thirty-Four

Mark Chester, the nephew of the elder Mr. Chester, had recently celebrated his eighteenth birthday. Sadly, his birthday had turned out to be a complete disaster. This was not unusual for the boy, seeing as how his entire life had just been a great series of unfortunate events.

All his life, he had always had the great misfortune of winding up in all the wrong places at all the wrong times. While living in Los Angeles, he had been caught in a ferocious earthquake and buried under the remains of his home for two days. Just as he was ready to give up hope, a passerby discovered him and saved his life. Mark's parents decided not to risk living any longer in a seismic area and moved to New York. Disaster found him there as well. As soon as he was hired for a part-time job in one of the World Trade Center towers, they were struck down by terrorists.

Only recently, just after his family moved to New Orleans from New York, a powerful hurricane ravaged the area. The entire city was flooded, and he had barely managed to escape alive. Of course, that was just his luck.

But why do I, like most of my relatives, constantly have bad luck? Why does it seem like we're all under a great curse? These were the things that continuously raced through Mark Chester's mind, although he had not discovered the answer to either question yet. With each passing day, however, he only felt more and more as if he would never find the answers. It seemed as if he was forever doomed to be a magnet for disaster.

The most recent unfortunate event was the fire he started at school. After the fire incident, he was expelled from school. Mark decided there was no reason to try to return to school, so he began looking for a job. But he quickly found there were few decent paying jobs for high school dropouts. Because Mark could not find any regular, well-paying work, he decided his best option would be to create his own job. Mark decided that he would case out expensive neighborhoods looking for opportunities to capitalize on his skills as a thief. He realized that many of the residents left their cars outside and unlocked at night. Some of them even left their garage doors open! And so, using this information as his springboard, he formulated a plan.

After leaving his car outside the subdivision for the night, he walked through a golf course that the houses bordered on and sneaked toward the first car. To his relief, the car was unlocked. The vehicle contained a large sum of cash and a video camera, all ready for the taking. Once he had ravaged the car for all its valuables, he moved on to the next one. This one wasn't locked either. Here, he fished out a wallet with several credit cards. Mark was just about to proceed to the next vehicle when the signal for a swift exit arrived. The distant wailing of police cars forced him to turn tail and run from the scene of the crime.

It turned out that a watchful resident had noticed Mark tampering with the cars. He had phoned the police because he suspected foul play. As the sirens grew louder, Mark ran back toward the golf course, dropping the evidence on his way. The camera and wallet tumbled behind him. Unfortunately, as was usual with the young man, the police managed to catch up with him before he got off the golf course. Mark was arrested and sentenced to three months in jail. It seemed his life had always been full of trouble, so he blamed his predicament on fate.

Mark was constantly bored during his three-month stay in jail, so he started reading the newspaper incessantly. He would read every word from the front page through the classifieds. One evening, just before his three months were up, Mark saw a help-wanted ad that read:

HELP WANTED
Young man needed for janitorial duties on cruise ship. Call Dream Line Cruises 1-800-555-1515.

Grinning darkly to himself, Mark decided to apply for the job as soon as he got out of jail. He thought about all the rich people who took cruises. As a janitor, he would have access to all their cabins where he could steal their jewelry and cash. Yes, this would be easy money, and he'd get paid to see the world. It was just the kind of job Mark had been dreaming of.

Mark Chester's janitorial duties provided him a master key to all of the guests' cabins. He made sure their bedrooms and bathrooms were spotless. The cruise line was glad to have him on staff because the passengers regularly commented on his excellent cleaning. They could not find a single particle of dust anywhere once Mark was through with their cabins. Unfortunately, as they neared the end of their cruises, they found more than dust vanishing.

When the passengers brought their suspicions to the captain, Mark would insist on their searching his cabin. He would plead with them, "Please search my cabin. I want you to see that I have not taken anything. Look everywhere. I assure you that you won't find a thing." Of course, the stolen objects were never found.

They really made it a little too easy for me, he thought to himself. He had been watching the latest passengers closely ever since they boarded the ship. He looked for every detail that indicated they might have something worth stealing. It had been easy to pick out the passengers who had the most valuable objects. The husbands were big tippers who liked to flash their cash. The wives had adorned themselves with their most expensive jewelry. He almost laughed out loud when he thought about how the women would wear their largest diamonds at dinner as they tried to out-dress each other. *Yes, they made it very easy. They practically invited me to take their valuables.*

On his most recent trip, Mark's big chance came when the ship docked in Thaifura. The passengers had gone to an elephant polo match and would stay on the island all day and through the evening. It gave Mark the perfect opportunity to search their rooms thoroughly without rushing. When the captain asked why it was taking longer than usual to clean the rooms, he simply replied, "I'd thought I'd take advantage of the passengers being gone all day to do some extra cleaning. It's sort of like spring cleaning." The captain loved it and thanked him for being so conscientious.

The first cabin he cleaned was for Vicky and her family. He searched through every drawer and square inch of floor but found nothing.

"Cheapskates . . ." he muttered angrily and moved on to his next assignment.

Unfortunately, the same disappointment awaited him in the next cabin. He went to the third cabin and hoped for better luck. He went through his usual routine and was about to leave when a green velvet bag in the top drawer of the nightstand caught his eye. He picked up the bag and peered inside. Mark could hardly contain himself. Jackpot! A silver necklace with a large emerald stone was curled inside with a pair of matching earrings and a bracelet.

Mark had never seen anything so beautiful. He pulled out the jewelry and admired it in the light. He marveled at his luck until he brushed his fingers against the large emerald stone. A dark foreboding sent a shiver down his spine. *Beauty and evil all in one,* he noted and slid the necklace into his pocket. Then, Mark checked his watch and realized he had to hurry if he was going to get through all of the cabins before the captain and the passengers returned.

Unfortunately, Taylor did not notice that her precious jewelry was missing until two days later. But by then, it was too late.

Chapter Thirty-Five

The sun did not shine in the morning. Unceasing rainfall had thundered against the ship all night long. Forked lightning repeatedly split the sky and wave after wave of thunder drowned everything in a great cacophony of noise. Hardly anyone slept, and the few who did had a restless sleep. Taylor barely got four hours of sleep the whole night. Her foremost worry was that the incredible typhoon was growing stronger by the second. As the captain had warned, it was the most violent storm to ever hit the Pacific. She was also worried about the emerald jewelry. She feared it was lost forever.

The captain arranged a search party consisting of willing volunteers and a few crew members to look for the jewelry, but nothing was found. What made it worse was the captain informed Taylor that her jewelry was not the first valuable to vanish. Other passengers had complained of similar disappearances. There was a thief among them, and the culprit had used this disaster as an opportunity to rip off the passengers. *Who would do such a thing?* Taylor pondered.

After being assured that the search for the missing items would continue, Taylor returned to her room. Erik, Kelly, Kyle, and Amanda soon joined her.

"So what should we do?" Kelly finally whispered.

"About what?" Kyle asked.

"About all of this. You know, the storm and Taylor's jewelry."

"There's nothing we can do," Taylor replied. "And anyway, I think that we should forget about the jewelry. Right now, the most important thing is finding a way to survive this storm."

Amanda looked up, her face full of fear. "I once saw on the Discovery Channel that typhoons are always supposed to weaken in strength after some time, but when I talked with the captain, he said this storm continues to increase in size and power. Even worse, he said that it seems to be tracking our ship. No matter which way he steers the *Dream Line*, the typhoon changes its path with the vessel."

There was a momentary silence among them. Then Erik, mouth gaping, exclaimed, "But what could that mean? Why would a typhoon be tracking our ship?"

"I think that's something we would all like to know," Amanda replied.

A great, empty silence filled the room. For a while, everyone was lost in his or her own thoughts and fears. Taylor kneaded her brain for ideas. *Why would a storm follow the Dream Line? What could it possibly want with us?* But she could find no reason that made sense. There was simply no explanation for what was going on.

She closed her eyes and pressed her palms against her eyes. *Think, think, think!*

Then Taylor heard a familiar voice slip into her mind. It brought comfort, peace, and power. She felt the assurance that everything would be all right. The voice whispered a single word: "Emerald." Then everything was silent again.

Emerald . . . emerald . . . emerald . . .

An instant later, Taylor realized what the voice meant and gasped, "Emerald! Of course! How could I have been so stupid?" Her friends looked at her in confusion, not sure what she was talking about.

Taylor turned to her friends and asked, "Do you remember what I said last night?"

"About the emerald jewelry being stolen?" Kelly questioned.

"Yes, but do you also remember how I said I wasn't sure when it was taken?"

"Yes!" the others replied in unison with growing excitement in their voices.

"I think that the jewelry was taken when the storm first appeared. Think about it. When the emerald jewelry vanished, a great typhoon came up out of nowhere and started following the *Dream Line*."

"And also," Erik added, "when we went to Ash Island, they told us it was going to be perfectly safe. But when we got there, a volcano that had been dormant for a thousand years erupted."

"Does that mean . . . " Kelly began.

"That . . . " Amanda continued.

"This is all happening . . . " Kyle picked up.

"Because of the missing jewelry," Taylor concluded.

"But how?" Erik asked.

Taylor looked at him with mystified eyes and replied, "That's the part I haven't been able to figure out yet. But if we're right, then we have to find that jewelry and get rid of it! It's the only way we can survive this storm!"

"There's just one thing that bothers me," Kelly said, thinking through what Taylor had said. "If the jewelry is causing all this trouble, why didn't anything happen before? I thought you had to wear the jewelry before anything bad happened."

"Maybe there's an exception. After all, this only began after the jewelry was stolen from me."

Amanda interrupted the conversation to add, "So what you're saying is that the reason all this bad stuff is happening is the jewelry was taken by someone who shouldn't have it? And now, because that person has it, the storm is rising up to take back the jewelry?"

"Exactly . . ." Taylor began, but she was cut off by a massive jolt. The five friends were thrown forward and onto the floor. Luckily, they landed on the carpet. Only Amanda, who had flown into the nightstand, had something to complain about.

"What was that?" Kelly cried out in fear.

Suddenly, the overhead lights dimmed, flickered, and died. The thunderous roar of the engine ceased and the ship descended into utter silence. Everything remained absolutely still for a few seconds. Then, they heard the sound of running footsteps. A few minutes later, even those stopped.

"Is everyone okay?" Erik yelled.

Kyle groaned somewhere to Taylor's right. "Yeah. . ."

"What happened?" Taylor heard Kelly's voice in the pitch-black darkness.

"I don't know," came Amanda's scared reply. "Maybe we should go ask the captain."

"Fine," Taylor replied, "but let's stay together. I don't even want to think of what could happen if we get lost on the ship."

Taylor placed her hands flat on the floor and began feeling her way to the door. *If only we had a porthole,* she thought to herself as she crept slowly along the floor. *But then again, with the sort of storm we're having, it wouldn't matter. The sky is pitch-black, too.*

After several painstaking minutes of bumping into random objects and people, she finally reached the door. Grasping the doorknob tightly, she opened the door wide to let the light in. Taylor stuck her head through the doorway and glanced along the hallway stretching to the left and right of her room. The emergency lights in the hallway were dim, but it was enough to see how to get to the stairway.

The others soon joined her in the hall. They exchanged frightened glances. Erik looked down the hallway and asked, "Are there emergency lights all along the ship? If not, we could get lost or trapped."

Taylor listened to the sounds of the others breathing softly, still thinking of what to do. Then Amanda got an idea. "Wait here," she ordered and dashed away down the hall.

"Amanda, no!" Taylor yelled angrily. "We all have to stick together!"

The girl turned around and smiled at her sister. "Hey, don't worry about me. I can take care of myself. Besides,

I've got a great idea! Trust me, okay?" And with that, she took off running down the hall.

"Amanda, get back here!" Taylor shouted, but realized it was no use. Amanda was already out of earshot. She stood up to go after her, but Erik caught her by the arm. "If you go after her, we'll really get separated. We should wait for her to come back here."

Taylor nodded solemnly. The other four sat down to wait for the girl, hoping that nothing bad would happen.

As she waited, Taylor thought back to everything that had happened on the trip. She thought of the dolphins, the elephant polo game, the wonderful time she had had with her friends, the bright sunlight on her hand . . .

It was only then that she realized that a shaft of light was pouring out from under the cabin door. It streaked across her skin, chilling her flesh wherever it touched her. Motioning for her friends to stay put, she pushed open the door and walked inside quietly.

The mirror in her room was glowing once more. Its surface reeled with smoky faces and soft voices filled the room. But this time, Taylor was not afraid. She approached the mirror and brushed her palm against the glass, but she instantly withdrew her hand, for the place she touched was covered with ice.

Suddenly, the faces in the mirror vanished, clearing the way for a single face. Taylor gasped when she recognized the smile and shining eyes of the countess. She was even more amazed when the woman spoke to her gently. It was only a whisper, softer even than the wind, but Taylor heard every word.

"You promised me that you would keep my necklace with you always. You have done well. I know this robbery is not your fault, but you must get the necklace, earrings, and bracelet back. They are not far from here, but be swift. The criminal shall soon escape. You cannot allow him to take the jewelry with him."

As suddenly as it had occurred, the mirror ceased giving forth light and the countess vanished. Taylor stepped back and quickly ran from the room. When her friends asked her about what had happened, she relayed every detail about the countess' request. They all agreed to try to stop the criminal if they got a chance.

Luckily, getting lost had not been on Amanda's to-do list. Soon, a beam of shining white light streamed down the hall. Amanda came after the beam. She had found a flashlight.

"I heard on the Discovery Channel that you should always bring a flashlight with you when going on a trip. You never know when you might need it!"

"You watch too much T.V.," Kelly teased, ruffling the girl's hair. Amanda pushed Kelly away with her hand and walked to the front of the group.

"Since I'm the one with the flashlight," she said proudly, "I get to walk in front."

"Go ahead!" Kyle told her. He winked at the others before adding loudly, "After all, it's always the person up front who gets eaten first by the aliens in movies. You know, the ones that stalk you in the darkness. I certainly don't plan to spend the rest of my vacation being digested. So you just go ahead and lead the way, kid."

They all saw fear creep into Amanda's wide eyes. She backed as far away as she could from the flashlight while still holding it and cast a fearful glance toward the shadows around them.

"On second thought," she said, her hand trembling as she handed the flashlight over to Kyle, "maybe you should lead us."

Kyle gave a satisfied chuckle and cast the bright beam down the hallway. The others crowded around the young man and the procession set off. The walk would have normally been dull, but under the present circumstances, only worries clouded everyone's mind. The hallway seemed infinitely long and the darkness around them seemed to be growing. Shadows danced on the walls, and the floor creaked beneath their feet. An occasional roll of thunder only added to the suspense. To make things worse, the flashlight and the emergency lights occasionally flickered or dimmed. Taylor noticed a connection. For some odd reason, the lights and the flashlight flickered at the same time. It was as if they were being influenced by an outside force greater than the storm . . .

After what seemed to be hours of walking, the flashlight's beam hit a set of stairs. "Where do these lead?" Kelly asked softly.

"I think they go to the main dining room," Erik replied.

"They lead either to the deck or to the dining room," Amanda said. "It all depends on which way we went down the hallway."

"Well, what are we waiting for? There's only one way to find out!" Taylor exclaimed, her voice loaded with determination, and she charged up the stairs.

When Taylor reached the top of the stairway, she saw that she had indeed arrived at the dining room. Cloth napkins and plates littered the dark hardwood floor, and several chairs were upturned. She called for the others to hurry. The captain and a group of passengers were gathered on the far side of the dining room. They seemed to be discussing something. Taylor was shocked, however, to see the captain with the passengers. *Why is the captain here instead of on the bridge?* she wondered as she joined the others to listen to the captain's words.

"Something strange has happened to the ship. My men are working to fix it as soon as possible," said the captain.

"What's going on?" Taylor asked from the back.

The captain looked at her in surprise. "Surely you've noticed by now that we've lost power. Right now, we're operating on our emergency generator."

"Yes, but why are you standing in the dining room with the passengers instead of on the bridge navigating us through this storm?"

The captain gave a short, mirthless laugh. "The ship's navigational system is no longer operational and the engines are dead."

"What?"

"The power failure has not only affected the lights, but also the entire power grid. Nothing on the ship is working except the emergency lights."

"So, does that mean . . ."

"That means we can't go anywhere until we fix the engines and restore the power. That is, *if* we can fix them. Right now, I don't even know why this is happening! Nothing on the ship is actually broken. If I were to take a wild guess, I would say that we have entered a Pacific version of the Bermuda Triangle."

Taylor's friends had been listening in the background. "Well," Kyle sighed, "at least the emergency lights and

Amanda's flashlight still work! It really can't get any worse than this."

In that instant, the emergency lights flickered, as did the flashlight in Kyle's hand. Then, the emergency lights shut down completely. The dining room plunged into darkness. The only sliver of light came from the flashlight, and even that was dim.

"You spoke too soon, Kyle," Taylor said sadly.

Amanda sighed. "Yeah, famous last words."

Taylor could feel bodies pushing pass her, and she heard people yelling wildly and calling for help. She felt her sister hug her around the waist and Taylor kneeled to hug her back. She heard the captain's voice shouting over the crowd, "Everyone, please calm down and stop moving! Stay where you are!"

The stampede subsided. Turning her eyes in the direction of the captain's voice, she waited for further instructions. The captain sighed deeply and said, "I realize we are in a very serious situation, but we can get through this if we work together. And I, for one, do not think that madness and confusion will solve anything. We need a plan, and any ideas would be appreciated. The most important thing is to stay calm. And Kyle," he motioned to the young man, "come up here with that flashlight."

Taylor heard whispers around the room. She dug deep into her mind for a plan. Suddenly, a man behind Taylor called out a question.

"What happened to the backup generators? I thought that those turned on and stayed on when there's no electricity."

"I don't know. Our generators are strong enough to sustain the ship for at least eight hours," the captain said. "Then again, strange things have been happening on this ship lately. Like I said before, nothing works now. Even things that aren't directly connected to the ship's power grid don't work."

The room fell quiet, and Taylor buried herself in thought once again. But it was her friend Kelly who got an idea first.

"Flashlights!"

Taylor heard the captain's voice again over the crowd. "What did you say?"

"I said, we can use . . ." But Kelly's reply was suddenly replaced by a gasp. The floor beneath them lurched and knocked everyone to the floor. *The storm is getting stronger,* Taylor thought as she stood up.

"What was the idea?" came the captain's voice once more.

"We can use flashlights while the power is out!"

"It's worth a try," the captain said. "Does anyone have a flashlight, other than the one Kyle has?"

Silence.

"Not one person on this entire ship except Kyle brought a flashlight with them?"

More silence. Then Amanda recalled something and exclaimed, "That janitor, Mark Chester, has flashlights! I remember them from when we searched his room after we discovered Taylor's jewelry was missing. We searched every corner of his cabin, and I remember there was a box of flashlights in his closet. We can ask him for them."

A woman from the crowd called out, "But who's going to go get them?"

There was a long silence while everyone wondered what to do. Finally, Kyle said, "Since I'm the one with the flashlight, I'll go."

"Then I'll go too!" Amanda exclaimed. "After all, it's my flashlight."

"Me three!" Taylor said.

"Count me in!" Erik yelled.

"Well, since all of my friends are going, I might as well go, too," Kelly said.

"I think," the captain said, "it would be better for one of my crew members to go. It might be dangerous for you kids."

Erik shook his head. "No. The crew have their hands full trying to repair the ship. We'll go together and protect each other. We'll be okay."

"Very well, then," the captain said. "Be very careful, though. And remember, we're all counting on you to get those flashlights."

"Don't worry," Taylor said. "We'll be back before you know it!"

"Excellent. But before you go, there's one more thing you'll need. Take this box of matches with you, just in case."

"Why would we need matches?" Taylor asked.

"If something happens to that flashlight, you'll need light to get back. Those matches won't give off much light, but at least you'll be able to see where you're going."

Taylor took the box of matches the captain offered her and put it in her pocket.

"Thank you," she said.

ॐ ॐ ॐ

A few minutes later, the five friends were huddled together in the dark corridor. They were standing in front of Mark's cabin door. After a long pause, Erik reached out and knocked on the door.

"Mark," Erik asked, "could you open the door?" The only reply they heard was silence.

"Mark," Erik repeated, "open the door! It's an emergency!"

When Mark didn't reply, Taylor turned the doorknob and found that it was unlocked. She pressed her hands against the door and watched it swing open quietly. The bare, hardwood floor creaked as they stepped into the room. Kyle swung the flashlight around to get a better look at their surroundings.

"So now that we're here," Kelly said, "lets just get the flashlights and go. They were in the closet, right?"

"Yes, I saw them on the floor of the closet," said Amanda.

Kyle went to the closet, but there was no sign of the flashlights. "They're not here," he said. "Start looking! Shout if you find the flashlights."

The five friends spread out around the cabin and started looking. They searched for a long time, but they came up empty-handed.

"Oh, I give up!" Amanda said at last. "We've looked everywhere, but the flashlights are nowhere to be found!"

"So what do we do now?" Erik asked.

"I know!" Amanda exclaimed. "When we came here to look for Taylor's jewelry, I also saw a huge pillar candle sitting on a shelf. We can bring that back to the captain."

"A lot of good one candle will do," chided Kyle.

"Since we can't find Mark or the flashlights, let's take the candle. It's better than nothing."

"Well . . . okay. I guess you're right. Now all we have to do is find the candle."

"There it is!" Amanda exclaimed, pointing towards a tall, white object sitting on a shelf. She rushed over to the shelf, nearly tripping on a newspaper that lay on the floor. With her fingers wrapped carefully around the base of the candle, she brought it back to the group. "Here you go," she said, giving the candle to Erik.

"Now all I need is one of the matches the captain gave you," Erik said, looking at Taylor.

Taylor fumbled for a moment with her pocket. She gingerly handed the box of matches to Erik. Everyone waited with baited breath as he struck a match against the box and brought it to the tip of the candle. The five friends watched with great anticipation as they awaited the blazing fire that would certainly erupt from the candle and illuminate the shadows around them and save them from their dark plight. The burning match touched the candle and . . . nothing. No light. No fire. No . . . anything.

Erik took out another match and tried again. Still nothing. Kelly cried out in anxiety and buried her face in Taylor's shirt. Taylor wrapped her arms around her best friend. Kyle sighed and turned away. But Erik shook his head and brought a third match up to the candle in a final attempt to light it.

This time, the candle sparked to life. A small plume of flame burst from the tip of the candle and cast dancing patches of light around the cabin. Everyone cheered and drew closer to the candle. Erik held the lit candle up in triumph and his four friends erupted in joyous noise. But that only lasted a second.

Suddenly, the ship gave an almighty lurch that knocked the five friends off their feet. Taylor crashed against the wall and slid painfully to the floor, tears welling in her eyes. *At this rate, the storm will destroy us all! Or, at the very least, it shall tear this ship apart!*

"We should get back to the dining room . . . fast!" Erik said, reaching out his hand to help Taylor to her feet.

"Yes," Taylor replied softly, "we should."

"Come on, then," Kyle said, running to the door. "I'll lead the way."

Amanda shuddered and drew close to her older sister. "Of course," she whispered. "Lead the way . . ."

When Taylor and her friends returned to the dining room, they found all of the passengers huddled together in the darkness. They placed the candle in a steel cage that was attached firmly to the floor to avoid a fire in case the candle tipped over.

The storm was now reaching critical levels. The waves were so strong that the ship was constantly tilting this way or that. Taylor grabbed a pipe to avoid sliding along with the ship. The other passengers around her did the same, each fastened onto some part or other of the ship.

From the center of the room, the candle cast great pools of light across the floor. The light gave hope to Taylor, and she wondered if the storm would end soon.

The passengers sat quietly in the dining room for quite some time. To Taylor, it seemed like an eternity. Nothing disrupted them except the constant jolting of the ship.

Taylor found herself staring at the candle. Her eyes traced the movement of molten wax from the top of the candle down to the base of the cage. *It really is fantastically beautiful,* she thought. *Nothing but the white of the candle, the dark black of the cage, and the tiny sparkle of silver at the base of the candle . . .*

Suddenly, she snapped out of her trance. *A tiny sparkle of silver at the base of the candle?* Just to make sure she wasn't mistaken, she looked again at the candle. Once again, she saw a flash of silver that seemed to come from a metal chain. *But how can that be?* After a few seconds, she voiced her suspicions to the captain.

Nodding, the captain slowly walked over to the candle. Taking care not to fall, he opened the cage and took out the candle. As he inspected the base of the candle, he noticed that a piece from the bottom of the candle had been cut out and reinserted. Using his pocket knife, he slowly pried out the plug of wax. A gasp escaped his lips, and he shook his head in disbelief when Taylor's emerald necklace fell into his hand.

"My necklace!" she cried in delight. "How on earth did it get there?"

But Taylor's necklace wasn't the only thing hidden in the candle. The captain took out Taylor's emerald earrings and bracelet as well as many more valuables from the candle as the passengers gathered around.

"My bracelet!" a woman beside Taylor called out.

"That watch is mine!" a man on the other side of the room exclaimed.

"Those earrings are mine!"

"My ring!"

"Hey, how did my broach get there?"

All these shouts and more echoed around the room. And with each new item the captain pulled out, the passengers became more and more amazed. Finally, once all the items had been taken out, the captain looked up and shook his head in horror. "I think that these are all of the missing items that everyone has been complaining about," he said. "Well, I think we can all guess how they ended up in this candle."

But no one got the chance to comment, for it was in that instant that Mark Chester ran through the doorway of the dining room and glanced around wildly. When he spotted the candle, he yelled, "That's mine! Give it to me!"

All heads turned to Mark. His hair was wild and disheveled, and he was scary-looking. His eyes were alive with sparks. Almost foaming at the mouth, he yelled again, "Thieves! How dare you go through my things?"

The captain snorted in disbelief. "Your things? All of this was stolen from these good people! Did you take all of these things?"

Mark gave a terrible laugh and grinned evilly. "Why, of course. How else do you think everything got in the candle?"

"But why, Mark?"

Mark grimaced angrily. "You wouldn't understand!" he exclaimed. "None of you would understand! And you won't believe the truth, either."

The captain furrowed his eyebrows and crossed his arms. "Try us."

Mark slowly walked toward the crowd of passengers. He stopped several feet from the captain and looked down at the floor. The young man took a deep breath and tears began to fill his eyes. "I heard this story from my mother. She always said there was a curse on our family. Maybe she was right. A long time ago, one of my ancestors worked as a servant for a powerful count. This man was blessed with two sons. But, much to his despair, his two children were as different as fire and ice. Two people born on opposite ends of the Earth could have been more similar than these two brothers. The elder son took on criminal ways early on in his life. The younger boy, on the other hand, became a monk. My ancestor disliked his older son because of the lifestyle he chose and tried to convince him to change. But the elder son grew angry and tired of his father's constant pleas and complaints, so he ran away from home."

Thunder rumbled loudly somewhere just outside the ship.

Mark continued, "Before he left, however, he stole the countess' prized emerald necklace. He would have escaped, but a girl and the count's son saw him from one of the towers and warned the guards that he was in the courtyard. In her anger, the countess placed a curse upon the thief."

Thunder beat his powerful drum again.

"Unfortunately, the elder son was not satisfied with just the necklace. One night, he tried to rob the castle again. A giant bronze statue of a woman holding a vase on her shoulder stood in one of the hallways in the castle. No one knew how it happened, but the next morning, the elder son was found dead in the hallway. His head had been pierced, and the vase from the statue was on the floor next to him."

An explosion of noise like no other before it came from outside. The typhoon was picking up strength.

"But the curse of the countess did not end with the criminal son. Since then, all of his descendants have suffered constant troubles."

"And it's all because of the necklace Chester's eldest son stole all those years ago," Taylor finished weakly.

Mark nodded sadly and turned away. Taylor could see his body shaking and wondered if he was sobbing. When Taylor looked at the passengers, she could tell that they were clearly moved and fascinated by his tale. She looked over at the hard face of the captain, and even there she could see a slight tinge of amazement and sadness. Her own heart might have swelled in pity for the young man, but her mind was too fraught with chaos and dark understanding for that now.

The story Mark had told paired up exactly with her dreams. He had said that the elder son was seen by a girl and the count's son from a tower. She and Erik had seen a man run across the courtyard that fateful night in her dreams. And the man pierced by a vase . . . Erik had led her from her room to see that terrible scene. *Then it all happened! My dreams really happened! They were dreams of the true past . . . my past!*

Yet, there was something suspicious about his tale.

"Even if you return all these items, I'll still have to report you to the police," said the captain. "Your story may be true, but that still doesn't justify your stealing."

Mark turned around again and his body stopped shaking. He began moving quietly toward the captain. Taylor thought she saw a dark glimmer in his eyes.

"Mark . . ." she began to say. The young man grinned menacingly. The dim light from the candle reflected off his shiny teeth.

"Um . . . captain . . ." Taylor started again.

"Yes?" said the captain, turning to face Taylor.

Unfortunately, that gave Mark his chance. He took a running leap and yanked the emerald necklace from the captain's hands. He laughed and exclaimed, "Well, if I can't have everything, at least I'll have this! How pathetic! All of you trusted me just like that! Well, let this be a lesson to you all: sob stories don't mean innocence!"

Mark's body started shaking again, but now Taylor could see that he shook not from regret for his actions, but because he was laughing at the passengers' stupidity. Mark grinned at the passengers once again and then dashed across the dining room and out the door.

A boiling well of hatred erupted inside Taylor. *So this was the criminal the countess told me about when I saw her in the mirror!* She closed her eyes and clenched her teeth tight. Her memories of the day when Chester's son stole the emerald necklace from the countess returned. The countess' face drifted to the surface of her mind, and she remembered the promise she had made to keep the necklace safe. It took her a single second to realize what she had to do. *I will not lose the necklace again,* she thought as she took off after Mark.

"Taylor," she heard her mother yell, "get back here this instant! Taylor!"

Eyes ablaze with courage and anger, she darted through the doorway and ran down the pitch-black staircase and then along the corridor beyond after Mark. She called back, "Don't worry, Mom. I'll be back soon."

She heard his footsteps echoing ahead. Her legs carried her with blinding speed after the criminal. *Faster . . . faster . . . I can't let him get away!* she thought and increased her speed. The walls were a dark blur. She was amazed that she did not bump into anything along the way. Everything around her was completely black. Finally, Taylor reached the foot of a set of stairs. Without any thought, she thundered up the stairs and shot out onto the deck.

Chapter Thirty-Six

The jet-black sky exploded in a raging blaze of fire and ice. Frozen rain crashed onto the deck, and flaming lightning criss-crossed the dark sky. Blasts of thunder added to the cacophony. Taylor narrowed her eyes and swept the deck with a piercing gaze. There, on the opposite side of the deck, stood Mark Chester, illuminated occasionally by a bolt of lightning in the dark. She let out a cry of fury that mingled in with all the other sounds of rage and anger and blaze. She had only a single thought in mind. *Get . . . Mark . . . Chester . . .*

Ignoring the rain pounding against her skin and the sizzling crackle of lightning and thunder overhead, Taylor took off across the deck. Unfortunately, the deck was slick with rain and her feet collapsed beneath her. But the girl only used this to her advantage. Because the stern of the ship had risen upwards, Taylor was now above Mark, and when she got down on her knees, she slid towards him with fiery speed. Her hair whipped out wildly behind her, and her clothes danced crazily around her.

But before she closed in on Mark, she heard a voice calling to her from behind. She turned to see Erik racing down the deck toward her. *He came after me*, Taylor realized. *He came . . .*

Remembering her mission, Taylor turned to where Mark had been moments before. She gasped when she saw that she was now hurtling towards empty railing! The criminal had moved while she was glancing back at Erik.

She used her feet to ricochet off the rail and towards Mark, who was now crawling nearly sideways along the railing. Taylor jumped on the young man, who in turn struggled and struck her hard across the face. A moment later, Erik joined Taylor and, together, they wrestled Mark to the floor of the deck. Realizing his defeat, he cringed and cried out, "Let me go!"

"Give me back the necklace!" Taylor demanded, her voice calm but with a steely edge. "I said, give me the necklace!"

"Why?"

"Because the necklace is evil! Because the necklace is cursed! This entire storm and all of our problems are because of that necklace! It's cursed and it must be hidden forever. Mark, you must give it to me! You must!"

"No!" Mark screamed, trying to break away. "No!"

But Erik and Taylor were too strong for him. They lifted the young man to his feet. Mark dangled weakly between them, his eyes blank now. His arms lay limp by his sides, and his head was tilted down. *We won!* Taylor thought happily. *It's all over now . . .*

But the sea was not through with them. The ship gave a massive jolt and the deck beneath their feet slipped sideways. Taylor, Mark, and Erik were all thrown off their feet again. Taylor crashed heavily to the deck, and Erik fell beside her. But Mark was thrown against the railing before collapsing onto the deck. Through the raging storm, she could see the glittering necklace in his fist.

Mark pushed himself up from the deck, holding his left side with one hand. He limped over to the railing, and he slowly lifted first one leg and then the other over the side. For a moment, Taylor did not understand why. But then she remembered . . . *there was a lifeboat on the other side of the rail!*

She wriggled forward slowly, carefully picking her way past jagged bits of wood from the deck that had been torn up by the storm. Mark had thrown himself completely over the railing now, and Taylor heard a dull thump. She heard the sound of wind as something fell through the air, and then a distant splash when the lifeboat struck the water.

Suddenly, another powerful wave broke against the side of the ship. The deck shifted again, and Taylor went sliding toward a stretch of railing that was below her, or, at least, where there should have been a rail. The railing had been torn away by the fury of the storm. Now, all that remained was a vast, gaping hole. Taylor screamed for all she was worth and tried to find something to cling to, but all her hands could reach was slick deck. Looking around frantically, she saw nothing to grab on to. The next second, she flew past the final stretch of rail. There was no longer anything between her and the raging, tossing, writhing sea below!

Taylor made a wild grasp for a piece of rail that had curled outward toward the sea. Her fingers managed to loop around the steel, but she continued to slowly slide downward. She closed her eyes tightly, wishing for it all to end. Taylor felt lost in a dark world of storm . . . and sea . . . and flame . . .

Just as she was about to fall into the raging sea, she felt powerful fingers circle around her wrist. They held her tightly and drew her upward and away from the churning waves. Taylor looked up and Erik's warm gaze met her eyes. She wrapped her other hand around the steel rail and helped him pull her onto the deck. Behind Erik, she saw her parents running toward them. Her mother was crying, and her father's face was contorted with fright. They wrapped their arms around Taylor, and she felt a lump rise in her throat. Running behind them were her friends and the other passengers, all looking frightened and curious.

At that moment, Taylor remembered Mark. She turned around and saw that the lifeboat had floated about fifty feet away from the ship. The dark waves rocked the little boat wildly, but Mark stood upright, glaring with contempt at the ship.

"So, you didn't catch me after all!" Mark laughed evilly. "You people . . . I despise you all!"

Erik clenched his teeth, but before he could make a retort, everyone gasped as the water around the little lifeboat began to bubble and froth. Worry clouded Mark's face. An instant later, the water shot straight up into the air in a vast column of white, icy rage and the lifeboat was lost to sight. At the same time, they heard a soul-shattering scream and a soft, distant plea. "Don't touch me! Let . . . me . . . go!"

Then the water dropped down from the sky to the sea in a great crack, and Mark was gone. He had simply vanished. The lifeboat, torn in half, began to sink beneath the raging black waves. The last bit of it they saw was a tiny corner of orange, but the dark water soon obscured even that.

Before any of them had a chance to understand what had happened, the now familiar ball of white fire rose from the black sea once more. It slowly drifted toward the ship, and the waves receded to allow it passage. The woman rose again from the flames, but this time, she stepped off the water and came to the ship's deck. She walked soundlessly along the broken boards to Taylor.

The girl was frightened, but when the woman motioned for her to follow, Taylor felt a wave of calm wash over her. As the woman turned to go, Taylor quickly moved to her side. The passengers backed away as the spirit of the white flames passed them, and they cast terrified glances at Taylor. When Taylor saw their looks, she smiled back, trying to dispel their fears.

When they reached the railing, the woman turned to look at Taylor. In a gentle voice, the woman asked, "Tell me, Taylor, who am I?"

"You're the spirit of the countess," Taylor said softly.

"And how do you know?"

Taylor's eyes opened wide and she smiled. "Because of what you told me. Because of that day at the sea when you left the castle. You wouldn't say why you were leaving, but you said that someday I would understand on my own. You told me to go and never forget."

"And you haven't forgotten. That's good. Now I have something for you—a gift, you might say." The countess reached into thin air and pulled from it a sparkling white ring with a single emerald stone. "Unlike the necklace, earrings, and bracelet, this has no magic, but it will go well with the set," she explained. "It is yours to keep forever."

Taylor breathed a word of thanks, slid the ring onto her index finger, and smiled at the countess. "I will never forget."

Her eyes shining with light, the countess passed over the railing and back to the sea. She turned back into fire, and the white flames were swallowed up by the dark water until they were lost beneath the waves.

The passengers standing on the deck gasped in terror at all that they had seen. But their first thoughts were of Mark Chester.

"He's gone now. I suppose the phantoms of the sea took him away," Alex said. "Maybe even those phantoms we saw that night in the sea. The white fires, I mean, or the woman who came to us now."

The captain shook his head sadly. "But we can't just abandon a man without even trying to save him." He ordered his men to watch the sea for any sign of Chester, but nothing was ever found of the young man.

The storm had now ceased to rage. The waves churned less and less, and the clouds began to break apart. The typhoon was finally gone.

"Taylor," Kelly asked as she approached her friend, "who was that?"

"An old friend," Taylor replied, smiling.

"Well, I guess there's no need for us to remain here," the captain said. "It would be best for us all to the return below deck. One of my crewmen just reported that the ship's power has been restored. My men and I will get the ship on its way as soon as possible."

The crowd of passengers followed the captain below deck, and soon only Erik and Taylor were left on deck. They exchanged no words, but instead stood side by side, leaning against the rail. When evening came and hung a yellow moon high above the sea, they did not leave the deck. The ocean of stars above rocked gently overhead and brought peace to them and to the rest of the Earth. The stars cleared away the remnants of the storm and covered the world with a new blanket of life. A soft sea breeze danced on their faces and played with their hair.

Erik gently hugged Taylor, slowly raised her chin, and touched his lips to hers. She closed her eyes and felt her soul seep outward into the kiss. Taylor had awaited this moment for so long, and she wanted to be lost forever in its depths. But alas, the terror and worries of the past few days struck her afresh. Taylor felt a great weariness pass over her. After all that had happened, it was finally time to rest.

Chapter Thirty-Seven

Taylor took a deep breath of fresh morning air. A whisper of wind ran through her hair as she stood, alone, on the *Dream Line*'s deck. Waves brushed gently against the hull as the ship rolled with the tide. The sky was clear and peaceful, and not a single sound shattered the silence. Taylor looked out over the railing and thought of all the things that had happened to her. *How strange, and yet how wonderful!* There had been frightening moments that had filled her with terror, and several times she had nearly given up, but in the end everything had turned out just fine. Most of all, she was glad it was all over.

Her eyes shifted to a half orb, fire against the watery horizon. *The sunrise out on the ocean is simply . . .* but she could find no word that could describe the raging emotions within her. The blaze of crimson against the icy sea and the burning red of the early sun filled her with strength and hope. Taylor gazed out at the boundless sea and thought of all the mysteries still to be uncovered by

the human race. It was all represented there, in the water, and in the sea. *Who knows what awaits us yet!*

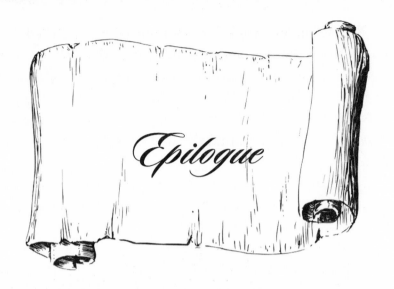

Epilogue

Andrew wiped his hands against his pants to rid them of the salty sea spray. He looked out over the ocean and grimaced slightly. They had been out at sea for two weeks now but had seen neither tooth nor fin of a single shark, even though it was migrating season. He and his fellow researchers were studying the patterns of shark migrations, but so far their efforts had been it vain. He slapped the water with his hand in frustration and got a face full of salt water in exchange.

Suddenly, one of the researchers let loose a strangled gasp and pointed, breathlessly, at a point far out toward the horizon. Andrew jumped up and ran over to stand by his colleague. His eyes traced the path of the man's outstretched finger. He wrung his hands in excitement and called for the boat to be steered closer to the area that everyone was now staring at. He could not believe what he saw.

The ocean was black with teeming bodies. Pointed fins jutted from the sea and cut slender paths through the water. Thousands of sharks darted around each other and swam with increasing speed toward some distant point only they knew. For a long time, there was not even a sparkle of blue water amid the mass, giving the scientists plenty to study.

Eventually, the sea cleared as the sharks moved on toward their destination. Andrew fell back in relief, glad their task was done. Now, to return home . . .

"Hey, Andrew, I think you might want to see this," a voice called out.

Andrew looked up curiously. "What is it, Albert?"

"Look," Albert replied and handed Andrew a pair of binoculars. He sighed, pressed the binoculars to his eyes, and turned them seaward. It took him a few moments to realize what he was seeing.

A single shark remained in the area—a great white. But this shark was not following the others. Instead, it just kept swimming in circles. Wondering what was wrong with the creature, Andrew called for it to be pulled on board for examination. The man behind the steering wheel nodded and drew the ship close to the restless shark.

The moment Andrew placed a hand on the shark's fin, it darted forward and bit at the ocean water. Its eyes full of fiery madness, it continued to swim around in its circle, teeth bared and ready for a war. Andrew cursed at the creature's stubbornness and took out a steel chain from within the ship's closet. He looped it carefully around the shark's head, lasso style, and began to drag it towards the ship. But the shark still had plenty of fight left, and it pulled against the chain in an attempt to drag the young researcher into the sea. Five more men grabbed the end of the chain and, together, they managed to haul the great white onboard. Before the shark could puncture the deck or a person with its massive teeth, they secured it tightly to the side of the ship.

Andrew examined the shark thoroughly but could not find anything wrong with it. *Perhaps there is something wrong inside,* he thought and asked for the sonogram machine. His fellow scientists wheeled one over immediately. He nodded his thanks and flicked the machine on.

At first, everything seemed to be in place. *Heart, gill chamber, brain . . . it's all there and undamaged. Everything looks healthy. What is the problem then?* At that moment, Andrew noticed something in the shark's stomach. *What's this?* Something strange was in the shark's belly. *Maybe I'm mistaken, but that appears to be some sort of necklace . . .*

Award-winning author Michelle Izmaylov lives in Atlanta, Georgia. She attends Alpharetta High School where she is in the ninth grade. Michelle's favorite things to do are writing, drawing and traveling to different countries. Her love of travel comes from her parents, Alex and Gina, who have been all over the world and speak four different languages. Michelle is fluent in Russian and is learning Spanish. Her mother, a professional musician, also instilled a love of classical music in Michelle.

Michelle's younger sister, Nicole, was the role model for the feisty Amanda. Her lovely Yorkshire terrier, Don, also had a role in the novel as Taylor's beloved pet.